"Decadent," He Pronounced. "Delicious."

Once again, Justin's low, ultrasensual tones sent an unfamiliar, unwanted and unappreciated chill down Hannah's already-quivering spine. At the same time, the spark of teasing devilment in his eyes caused a strange, melting heat deep inside her.

Hannah resented the sensation, but to her chagrin, she felt every bit as attracted to Justin as she was wary of him. All he had to do was look at her to make her, in a word, sizzle.

Dammit.

It had been a long time since Hannah had warmed to a man and she had certainly never *sizzled* for one. But innate honesty compelled her to admit to herself that she did indeed sizzle for Justin.

And she didn't like it at all.

Dear Reader,

Welcome to another scintillating month of passionate reads.
Silhouette Desire has a fabulous lineup of books, beginning
with *Society-Page Seduction* by Maureen Child, the newest
title in DYNASTIES: THE ASHTONS. You'll love the
surprises this dynamic family has in store for you…and each
other. And welcome back *New York Times* bestselling author
Joan Hohl, who returns to Desire with the long-awaited
A Man Apart, the story of Mitch Grainger—a man we
guarantee won't be alone for long!

The wonderful Dixie Browning concludes her DIVAS WHO
DISH series with the highly provocative *Her Fifth Husband?*
(Don't you want to know what happened to grooms one
through four?) Cait London is back with another title in
her HEARTBREAKERS series, with *Total Package.* The
wonderful Anna DePalo gives us an alpha male to die for,
in *Under the Tycoon's Protection.* And finally, we're proud
to introduce author Juliet Burns as she makes her publishing
debut with *High-Stakes Passion.*

Here's hoping you enjoy all that Silhouette Desire has to
offer you…this month and all the months to come!

Best,

Melissa Jeglinski

Melissa Jeglinski
Senior Editor
Silhouette Desire

Please address questions and book requests to:
Silhouette Reader Service
U.S.: 3010 Walden Ave., P.O. Box 1325, Buffalo, NY 14269
Canadian: P.O. Box 609, Fort Erie, Ont. L2A 5X3

JOAN HOHL

A MAN APART

Published by Silhouette Books
America's Publisher of Contemporary Romance

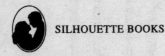

SILHOUETTE BOOKS

ISBN 0-373-76640-8

A MAN APART

Copyright © 2005 by Joan Hohl

This edition published by arrangement with Harlequin Books S.A.

Visit Silhouette Books at www.eHarlequin.com

Printed in U.S.A.

Books by Joan Hohl

Silhouette Desire

A Much Needed Holiday #247
*Texas Gold #294
*California Copper #312
*Nevada Silver #330
Lady Ice #354
One Tough Hombre #372
Falcon's Flight #390
The Gentleman Insists #475
Christmas Stranger #540
Handsome Devil #612
Convenient Husband #732
Lyon's Cub #762
†Wolfe Waiting #806
†Wolfe Watching #865
†Wolfe Wanting #884
†Wolfe Wedding #973
**A Memorable Man #1075
**The Dakota Man #1321
**A Man Apart #1640

Silhouette Romance

A Taste for Rich Things #334
Someone Waiting #358
The Scent of Lilacs #376
Carried Away #1438
   "Logan Objects"

*Desire trilogy
†Big, Bad Wolfe Series
**The Graingers

Silhouette Special Edition

Thorne's Way #54
Forever Spring #444
Thorne's Wife #537

Silhouette Intimate Moments

*Moments Harsh,
   Moments Gentle* #35

Silhouette Books

†*Wolfe Winter*

Silhouette Summer Sizzlers 1988
"Grand Illusion"

Silhouette Christmas Stories 1993
"Holiday Homecoming"

Silhouette Summer Sizzlers 1996
"Gone Fishing"

JOAN HOHL

is the *New York Times* bestselling author of over forty books. She has received numerous awards for her work, including the Romance Writers of America's Golden Medallion award. In addition to contemporary romance, this prolific author also writes historical and time-travel romances. Joan lives in eastern Pennsylvania with her husband and family.

Melissa & Tara
Gee, it's good to be back home again.

One

Justin Grainger was a man apart—and he liked it that way. He was content with his life. Possessing a nearly uncanny affinity for horses, he was satisfied with his work of running his isolated horse ranch in Montana.

But Justin was not a hermit or even a true loner. He enjoyed the easy camaraderie shared with his ranch hands and his foreman, Ben Daniels. And though Justin had never again wanted a woman on the property, since his failed marriage five years before, he had accepted the presence of Ben's new young wife, Karla. She had been the former personal assistant to Justin's brother, Mitch, who managed the family-owned gambling casino in Deadwood, South Dakota.

Justin had other family members he occasionally visited. His parents, retired now in Sedona, Arizona, were both still healthy and socially active. His sister, Beth, as yet unmarried, was off doing her fashion thing in San Francisco. And his eldest brother, Adam, headed up various family businesses from their corporate offices in Casper, Wyoming.

Adam was married to a lovely woman named Sunny, whom Justin had set out to tolerate in the name of family unity and had quickly come to admire, respect and love almost as much as his own sister. Adam and Sunny had a baby daughter, Becky, whom Justin quite simply adored.

On occasion Justin even spent recreational time with an accommodating woman—no strings attached. And that suited him fine. He claimed that horses were much easier to deal with, less contentious and argumentative, thus easier to talk to and get along with.

Although, these days, after a long, hot work-filled summer, a busy autumn, and winter just settling in, Justin was a bit restless and didn't grumble too much when he received an urgent and demanding phone call from Mitch the week before Christmas.

"I need you to come to Deadwood," Mitch said, in his usual straightforward way.

"Yeah? Why?" Justin replied, in his usual dry, less-than-impressed manner.

"I'm getting married, and I want you to be my best man," Mitch shot back. "That's why."

As an attention getter, his brother's explanation was a winner, Justin conceded…to himself. He never had conceded much of anything—except absolute loyalty and devotion—to any one of his siblings.

"When did you lose it, Mitch?" he asked in soft tones of commiseration.

"Lose what?" Mitch sounded slightly baffled.

Justin grinned. "Your mind, old son. You must have lost it if you're going to take the marital plunge."

"I haven't lost my mind…old son," Mitch retorted, a trace of amusement undermining his rough voice. "Trite as it might sound, it's my heart I've lost."

There was no way Justin could let his brother's remark pass without comment. "No 'might' about it," he drawled, enjoying himself. "That is trite. Sappy, too."

Mitch laughed. "I don't know what to tell you, bro," he said, suddenly dead serious. "I'm way deep in love with her."

Oh, yeah, Justin thought, hearing the heartfelt note in his brother's voice. Mitch was seriously serious. "It's Maggie Reynolds. Right?"

"Yes...of course."

Of course. Justin wasn't surprised, not really. A faint smile tugged at his lips. In fact, after all the rave reviews he'd heard from Mitch about Ms. Reynolds ever since she'd replaced Karla as his personal assistant, Justin should have been expecting the marriage announcement.

"Well?"

Mitch's impatient voice sliced across Justin's thoughts. "Well what?" he asked.

Mitch sighed loudly, and Justin managed to contain a burst of laughter.

"Will you be best man at my wedding?"

"Might as well," Justin drawled. "Why change the status quo now...as I always was the best man, anyway."

"In your dreams, maybe," Mitch said amiably going along with the old joke. "Because you're never gonna live long enough to see that day while you're awake."

"Ha! Don't bet the casino on it."

"As if…" Mitch made a snorting sound; he never gambled on anything, never mind the family owned casino. "You know damn well I never…"

"Yeah, yeah. I do know, so spare me the drill. When do you want me in Deadwood?"

"We've set the date for the first Saturday in the new year. But you could come for Christmas," Mitch suggested, cautiously hopeful.

"I don't think so." Justin slanted a wry look at the tall, glittery tree placed in front of the wide living room window. The tree—along with other assorted holiday decorations—was a concession to Ben's new bride. "You know I'm not—"

"Into Christmas," Mitch finished for him. "Yes, I know." He heaved a tired-sounding sigh. "This Christmas it'll be five years since Angie took off with that sales rep. Don't you think it's time to put it behind you, Justin, find a nice, decent woman and—"

"Back off, Mitch," he growled in warning, closing his mind to the memory of that bitter winter. "The only woman I'll be looking to find won't be either too nice or too decent, just ready and willing."

"Tsk, tsk," Mitch said, clicking his tongue in disapproval. "I do hope that if you're thinking of looking while you're here in Deadwood, you'll be discreet about it."

"Don't want me to shock the sensibilities of the future missus, hmm?" Justine taunted.

"My future missus and Ben's missus and Adam's missus," Mitch taunted right back. "Not to mention the sensibilities of our mother and sister."

"Ouch." Justin laughed. "Okay. I'll be extra discreet…even circumspect."

Mitch chuckled. "Whatever."

"By the way, is Karla going to be matron of honor?"

"Well…yes, but there'll be two of them."

"Two what?"

"Well, two attendants," Mitch said. "Maggie's best friend will be coming from Philadelphia via Nebraska to be Maggie's *maid* of honor."

"Philadelphia via Nebraska?"

"She lives in Philadelphia," Mitch explained. "That's where Maggie's from, you know."

"Yeah, I know, but…where does Nebraska come in?"

"Hannah's originally from Nebraska, and she'll be visiting her family before coming on to Deadwood."

"Hannah, huh?" Justin had an immediate image of an old-fashioned female to fit the old-fashioned name—prim, proper, virginal and probably plain.

"Yeah, Hannah Deturk."

Add *prudish* to the list.

"And you'd better be nice to her," Mitch warned.

"Of course I'll be nice to her. Why the hell wouldn't I be nice to her?" Justin said, genuinely hurt by his brother's warning, by the idea that Mitch felt it necessary to issue the warning.

"Well…" Mitch's tone was now conciliatory. "You've never made a secret about how you feel about women, and I just don't want anything to upset Maggie."

"You sound as smitten as Ben," he said. "You really do have it bad, don't you?"

"I love her, Justin, more than my own life," Mitch admitted in a quiet, but rock-solid tone.

"I hear you, and I promise I'll behave." He knew he'd never felt like that about a woman, not even his ex-wife, Angie, and was certain he never would.

Hell, he never wanted to experience that kind of intense emotion for any woman, Justin thought minutes later, frowning as he cradled the receiver. That path only led to pain.

First Ben and Karla, now Mitch and Maggie, he mused, staring into space, and all within one year.

Hmm. While Justin wasn't fanciful, he did wonder if there was some type of aphrodisiac in Deadwood's water, or maybe it was the atmosphere in the casino, some sort of love and marriage spell.

The day after Christmas, Justin set off for Deadwood, convinced he was impervious to anything like a spell or potion. He'd learned his lesson.

Hannah Deturk had not been exactly thrilled to be leaving Philadelphia at the end of the third week of December, of all times of the year, for the upper Midwest. South Dakota via Nebraska. To Hannah Deadwood, South Dakota was the back of beyond and, if possible, even more remote than the area of Nebraska where she had been born and raised.

After graduating college and relocating, first to Chicago, which was too windy, then to New York City, which was too big, and finally settling into

Philadelphia, Hannah had vowed that other than brief visits home to visit her folks, she would never go back to that desolate part of the country. She certainly wouldn't travel there in the winter months of November, December, January, February and March, and she even considered October, April and May pretty chancy.

Only a request by her parents or, as was the case, the marriage of her dearest friend, Maggie, could induce Hannah to take the three hard-earned vacation weeks she had allotted herself and spend them in Deadwood, South Dakota, of all places.

She didn't even gamble, for goodness sake, had never even visited the casinos in Atlantic City, a mere hour or so drive down the Atlantic City expressway from Philly.

And yet when Maggie had called her to tell her she was getting married in January and asked Hannah to be her maid of honor, Hannah hadn't so much as entertained a thought of refusing.

So, a few days into the new year, after spending Christmas with her family in Nebraska, Hannah found herself on the road, steering a leased four-wheel-drive vehicle through a blessedly light fall of snow, heading for Deadwood.

It was dark, and the snowfall heavier when

Hannah finally arrived in the town made legendary by its historical reputation of being wide-open and the larger-than-life characters of Wild Bill Hickok and Calamity Jane.

Those days were long-gone, as were the infamous pair. Other than having legal gambling casinos, Deadwood looked to Hannah much like any other small upper Midwest town.

She missed Philadelphia, where it would be evening rush hour and the traffic would be horrific. She even missed that.

Then again…perhaps not.

Smiling wryly, Hannah peered through the windshield to look for the turnoff Maggie had indicated in her directions. A few minutes later she brought the vehicle to a careful stop in front of a large Victorian house that had been converted into apartments.

No wonder Maggie had fallen in love with the house, Hannah thought, stepping out of the Jeep to stare through the swirling snow at the old mansion that had once been the Grainger family home. It was an imposing sight, and conjured images of a bygone era of grace and style.

"Hannah!"

Hannah blinked back into the present at the excited sound of Maggie's voice calling her name. Her coatless friend was dashing down the veranda steps toward her.

"Maggie!" Hannah flung out her arms to embrace her friend. "Are you nutty, or what?" she asked, laughing, as she stepped back to gaze into her friend's glowing face. "It's snowing and freezing out here."

"Yes, I'm nutty." Maggie laughed with her. "So nutty and crazy in love, I don't feel the cold."

"Got your love to keep you warm, do you?" Hannah dryly teased.

"Yes…yes." Despite her heartfelt assertion, Maggie shivered. "I can't wait for you to meet him."

"I'm looking forward to it," Hannah said, grasping Maggie's arm to lead her toward the house. "But meanwhile let's get inside, where I hope it's warm."

"Well, of course it's warm." Maggie flashed a grin. "Even up in my nest on the third floor."

Releasing her hold on Maggie's arm, Hannah turned back to the car. "You go on ahead, I'll just grab my bags and be with you in a minute."

"Did you bring your dress for the wedding?" Maggie called from the shelter of the veranda.

"Of course I did," Hannah yelled back over the

open trunk lid, shivering as the sting of wind-driven snow bit into her face. "Now go into the house."

A half hour later, her bags unpacked, the special dress she had frantically shopped for before leaving Philly hanging on a padded hanger to de-wrinkle, Hannah sat curled on the cushioned seat in the bay window alcove in Maggie's warm "nest," her hands cradling a steaming cup of marshmallow-topped hot chocolate.

She took a careful sip, and winced. "Mmm...delicious. But very hot. I scorched my tongue."

Maggie laughed. "It's supposed to be hot." Her eyes danced with amusement. "That's why it's called *hot* chocolate."

Hannah's pained expression smoothed into a gentle smile. It was so good to hear her friend laugh again, see the glow of happiness in Maggie's face that had replaced the bitter hurt of betrayal of the previous summer.

"You really are in love this time," Hannah said, taking another careful sip. "Aren't you?"

"Yes...though I wouldn't have believed it possible mere months ago...I really am in love." Maggie heaved a contented sigh. Her eyes took on a dreamy look. "Mitch is so wonderful, so, so..."

"Everything Todd was not?" Hannah inter-jected, her normally husky voice lightened by ex-pectation.

"Todd who?" Maggie asked with assumed in-nocence.

Hannah grinned, finally convinced her friend was back on track at last. "Oh, you know, Todd what's-his-name, the jerk you were engaged to marry. The same jerk who eloped with his boss's daughter."

Maggie grimaced. "Oh, *that* jerk. Yes, Mitch is everything Todd was not." Her lips formed a soft smile. "And a whole heck of a lot more."

"Good." Allowing herself to fully relax, Han-nah settled more comfortably into the corner of the alcove. Smiling, she studied her friend's radiant face. "You really are genuinely in love this time," she murmured in tones of wonder. "Aren't you?"

Maggie laughed. "Didn't I just answer that question moments ago? Yes, Hannah, I am deeply, genuinely, madly, desperately, deliriously…

"Okay, okay," Hannah broke in, holding up her hands and laughing. "I believe you."

"About time." Maggie laughed with her. "More hot chocolate? A cookie?"

"No, thank you." Hannah shook her head. "I still

have some chocolate—" she grimaced "—and I've already had too many cookies. They're delicious."

"Karla baked them."

Hannah frowned. "Karla?" Then, remembering, she said, "Oh, the woman whose job you took over, the one who's going to stand as matron of honor."

"Mmm." Maggie nodded. "She loves to cook, and baked these for Christmas. She brought some with her for us."

"That was thoughtful of her." Hannah smiled. "So, she's here already, too. I'm eager to meet her."

"Yes, she's here in Deadwood. Karla and her husband, Ben, and the baby." Maggie laughed. "Matter of fact, the whole gang's here."

"Gang?" Hannah lifted one perfectly arched brow.

"Yes, Mitch's family," Maggie explained. "They arrived in dribbles and drips over the past two days…"

"Dribbles and drips," Hannah interrupted, laughing. "Your Pennsylvania Dutch country origins are showing."

"Whatever." Maggie shrugged. "Anyway, they're here. Mitch's parents, two brothers, one alone, one with his family, and his sister. You'll meet them Friday evening at the rehearsal, and get to know them a little at dinner afterward."

"Dinner?" Hannah swept the room with a skeptical glance. "Where?"

"Mitch made arrangements for dinner at the Bullock Hotel."

"Oh." Naturally, Hannah hadn't a clue where the Bullock Hotel might be located, but it didn't matter. "And is that when I'll meet your Mitch?" Now, that did matter, a lot. She had witnessed the hurt and humiliation inflicted on Maggie by her former fiancé. Hannah had never been able to bring herself to trust or like the too-smooth Todd. Subsequently, to her dismay, her suspicions about him had proved correct.

"No." Maggie shook her head. "You'll meet Mitch tonight. He's going to stop by later. Though he's eager to meet you—I've told him so much about you—he wanted to give us some time alone together, to catch up." Her eyes softened. "He's so considerate."

Hmm, I'll be the judge of that, Hannah mused. But it sure sounded like Maggie did have it bad. "How does it really feel? Being in love, I mean?"

"All the things I mentioned before…and perhaps a little scary, too."

"Scary?" Hannah was at once alert, her protective instincts quivering. Was this Mitch Grainger a bully? She couldn't imagine her independent friend falling for a man who would intimidate her, but then again, Maggie had been about to marry that deceitful jerk Todd.

"Well, maybe not exactly scary," Maggie said, after giving it some thought. "It's all so new and sudden, and almost too exciting, too thrilling. You know how love is."

Whoa, Hannah thought, serious stuff here…. Too exciting? Too thrilling? Now she really couldn't wait to meet the man. "Actually, no," she admitted, wryly. "I don't know."

Maggie blinked in astonishment. "You're kidding."

"No, I'm not."

"You've never been in love? What about that guy you dated in college?"

"Oh, I thought I was in love," Hannah said. "Turned out it was a combination of chemistry and itchy hormones, commonly called lust." Her tone was dry, her smile self derisive.

"But…since then…?" Maggie persisted.

"Nope." Hannah swallowed the last of the chocolate; it had gone as cold as her love life…or lack of same. "There were a couple of infatuations, some sexual activity, but not much. There was one brief and I thought promising relationship I never told you about. But it really never got off square one, so to speak." She shrugged. "Nothing even remotely resembling what you've described."

"Oh, too bad. All this time we've known each other, and I never knew, never even guessed… you've always been so closemouthed about your personal life."

Hannah laughed. "That's because I didn't have one, at least nothing that warranted discussion."

"I never imagined…" Maggie sighed, then brightened. "Oh, I can't wait for you to fall in love someday, experience this excitingly scary champagne-bubbly feeling."

"I'm not sure I want to." Hannah slowly moved her head back and forth.

"Not want to?" Maggie exclaimed, surprised. "But…why not?"

"Because…" Hannah hesitated, carefully choosing her words so as not to offend her friend by voicing doubt. "I don't think I want to expose myself to that degree."

"Expose yourself?" Maggie frowned in confusion. "I don't get your point. Expose yourself to what?"

"That sort of emotional vulnerability," she said.

Maggie's amusement showed with her easy laughter. "You're wacko...you know that? Don't you realize that if I'm emotionally vulnerable, stands to reason Mitch is, too?"

"I suppose so," Hannah murmured. But is he? She kept the question and her doubts to herself. She had always considered herself a pretty good judge of character, and she had been right about Todd.

Wait and see, she told herself, lifting an eyebrow in question when Maggie, suddenly frowning, nibbled on her lower lip in consternation.

"Is something wrong?"

Maggie lifted her shoulders in an indecisive shrug. "Not really...it's just..."

"Just?" Hannah prompted.

Maggie sighed. "Well, I think maybe I should give you a heads-up on the best man, Mitch's brother, Justin."

"A heads-up?" Hannah grinned. "Why, is he some kind of ogre or monster?"

Maggie grinned back. "No, of course not. It's just...well...he's different, a little rough around the edges, not nearly as polished as Mitch or their oldest brother, Adam."

"Like, crude?" Hannah raised an eyebrow.

"No, no." Maggie shook her head. "Just a little

brusque. I understand he is something of a loner, thinks women are good for one thing only."

"I don't think I need ask what the one thing might be," Hannah drawled. A thought occurred that brought a glint of anger into her eyes. "Was this 'loner' brusque and perhaps a little rude to you?"

"Heavens no!" Maggie exclaimed on a laugh. "Actually, he was quite civil, really very nice."

"Then, how do you know that he—"

Maggie interrupted. "Because Mitch gave me a heads-up." She laughed. "He told me I should tell him at once if Justin said one word out of line." Her laugh turned to a giggle. "Mitch said if he did, he'd mop the casino floor with him. Which, after I met him, I thought was hilarious."

Thoroughly confused, Hannah was about to demand a fuller explanation when Maggie glanced at the clock, pushed her chair away from the table and stood.

"I think I'd better get dinner started," Maggie said. "I don't know about you, but I'm getting hungry. And I told Mitch we'd have coffee and dessert with him."

"Okay. I'll help," Hannah said, stretching as she stood.

"But…you're my guest," Maggie protested. "The first one I've had in this apartment."

"Guest, shmest," Hannah retorted. "I'm not a guest, I'm a friend…your best friend. Right?"

"Right." Maggie gave a vigorous nod, then qualified, "After Mitch, of course."

Oh, brother, Hannah thought. "Oh, of course," she agreed with a smile, skirting around the table. "What's on the menu?"

"Pasta."

Hannah rolled her eyes. "What else?" Being Maggie's second-best friend, she was well aware of her passion for past dishes. "What kind?"

"Penne with snow peas, baby carrots, walnuts and a light oil-balsamic-vinegar sauce."

"Yummy." Hannah's mouth watered. "And dessert?"

"A surprise." Maggie's eyes gleamed.

"Oh, come on," Hannah groused, grinning.

Maggie shook her head. "All I'll tell you is that Karla showed me how to make it." Her eyes now sparkled with a teasing light. "And it's a delight," she finished on a suspicious-sounding giggle.

After their fabulous meal, Hannah leaned back in her chair. "That was wonderful," she said, sighing with repletion.

"Thanks." Maggie arched an eyebrow as she rose to start clearing the table. "How's the career progressing?"

"Right on schedule. I figure by the time I'm eighty or ninety, I'll be the best damn consultant in the entire marketing industry," Hannah drawled, rising to help clean up.

Maggie shot a frown at her. "No, seriously, how is it going for you?"

"Very well, actually," Hannah answered, helping Maggie to fill the dishwasher. "I gave myself a raise by raising my fee in November. Not one of my clients objected. My end-of-year earnings have put me into a higher income tax bracket, and I don't even mind."

"That's great," Maggie exclaimed, rewarding her with a hug. "Congratulations."

"Thank you," Hannah said simply, going on to candidly admit, "At the risk of sounding arrogant, I'm rather pleased with myself at the moment."

"And why not?" Maggie demanded, her hands planted on her slender hips. "You should be pleased and delighted. You've worked your butt off getting yourself established. I know. I was there. Just as you've always been there for me. Remember?"

Hannah smiled, recalling the day the previous June when she had walked into Maggie's apartment to witness her friend slashing the exquisitely beautiful, extremely expensive wedding dress to shreds. "Remember? How could I forget all the pain—and fun—we've shared?"

"Well, while you're here, let's just remember the fun, and say to hell with the pain. Deal?"

Hannah laughed. "Deal."

They shared a hug and, sliding an arm around each other's waists, strolled to the other side of the room to settle back down on the window seat behind the table, chattering away while they waited for Mitch.

With each passing moment, Maggie's face took on a becoming glow, her eyes shining with anticipation. And with each of those moments, Hannah felt her own anticipation rise, as she wondered what kind of man this Mitch Grainger must be. Not to mention his enigmatic brother.

Two

Having listened to Maggie rave, through several long-distance phone calls, about how handsome, exciting, wonderful and flat-out sexy her employer and fiancé was, Hannah was prepared for the visual impact of Mitch Grainger.

So, when he arrived at the apartment a half hour later, she was neither surprised nor disappointed. Mitch appeared to be everything Maggie claimed him to be and then some. His manner was polite. He was gentle and tender with Maggie, and the perfect gentleman toward Hannah.

She couldn't help but notice that every time Mitch looked at Maggie, his eyes gleamed with near adoration, joy and male sexual hunger. Strangely, that gleam of light gave Hannah an odd little twist in her chest.

Surely not envy of Maggie and the emotions the mere sight of her so obviously induced in Mitch?

Envy? Of her very best friend? The very idea was both confusing and shaming. Hannah might have examined her unusual feeling more closely if there had been just the three of them around the small table.

But Mitch had not come to the apartment alone.

While Hannah had been prepared for Maggie's fiancé she hadn't at all been prepared for the impact of Mitch's older brother, Justin.

And what an impact he made. Hannah felt the reverberations in every molecule of her being— felt it and resented it. In looks, the brothers were quite similar, but altogether different in attire.

Mitch was dressed in a navy-blue business suit, ice-blue shirt, a striped, pale-blue and grey tie and a long gray obviously cashmere coat, the walking picture of the conservative businessman. Justin, on the other hand, had removed a brown, well-worn Stetson and shrugged out of a deep-collared suede jacket. Beneath his coat he wore a blue chambray shirt tucked into faded low-slung jeans plastered to his slim hips and long legs to cover the tops of smart-looking boots.

Justin Grainger towered over Hannah's five foot ten by seven and a half inches. His raw-boned frame was rangy but muscular, a tower of powerful masculinity.

At once, Hannah understood how Maggie had found it hysterical when Mitch threatened to mop the casino floor with his brother if he said one word out of line. While Mitch appeared quite capable of wiping the floor with most men, she knew his brother wasn't one of them.

Justin Grainger had dark hair, streaked with silver at the temples, and a little long at the nape. His eyes were gray, cold as the North Atlantic in January, sharp as a bitter wind, yet aloof and remote. And every time he turned his cold, calculating, but somehow tinglingly sexy sharp-eyed gaze on Hannah, she felt a chilling thrill from the tingling top of her head to the curling tips of her toes.

Hannah's immediate assessment of the two brothers was that Mitch was forceful and dynamic, whereas Justin was a silent but simmering volcano of leashed sexuality, with the potential to erupt without warning all over any innocent, unsuspecting female to cross his path.

Fortunately, having survived that one unsuccessful and unsettling relationship two years before—a relationship in which she had been burned so badly she hadn't even confided in Maggie about the affair or aftereffects—Hannah was neither innocent nor unsuspecting. To be sure, she was suspicious as all get-out.

On Maggie's introduction, Hannah accepted Mitch's proffered hand first. It was warm, his grip polite. But she barely registered his greeting, since all she could hear was the sound of static electricity as she took Justin's extended hand. She not only heard it, she felt it zigzag from her palm to every particle of her body.

Hannah slid a quick glance toward Maggie and Mitch only to find that they had moved across the room to the hallway closet to put away the men's coats.

"Miss Deturk."

That's all he said. Her name. Not even her first name. His voice was low, disturbingly intimate. Hannah's hand felt seared. She hadn't realized his fingers were still firmly wrapped around hers. She turned her gaze back to his, her mouth going dry at the sight of tiny flames flickering in the depths of his cold gray eyes.

Feeling slightly disoriented, and resenting the sensation, she slid her hand free, murmuring, "Mr. Grainger."

"Justin."

"If you wish." She inclined her head, feeling like an awkward teenager, not having a clue she gave the impression of a haughty queen condescending to acknowledge one of her lowest subjects.

A smile shadowed his masculine, tempting lips. "May I call you Hannah?"

Oh, hell, she thought. His voice was even lower, more intimate, and too damn beguiling. Certain her brain had been rendered into nothing more than a small blob, Hannah could manage only to parrot herself.

"If you wish."

"Well, ready for dessert?" Maggie's bright voice dissolved the strange misty atmosphere seemingly surrounding her and Justin Grainger.

Thank heavens for small mercies, Hannah thought, turning away from him.

"Do you have coffee?" Mitch asked.

"Of course." Maggie crossed to the small kitchen area.

Grateful for a moment's respite from Justin's nearness, Hannah hurried after Maggie to help. She served the coffee, careful not to look directly at him. She thought she had herself under control when she again seated herself next to him at the table.

The moment she was settled, she knew she was wrong.

Beneath Justin Grainger's keen gaze, Hannah's enthusiasm waned for the coffee and the surprise dessert promised by Maggie.

"What is it?" Mitch asked, eyeing the dessert dish Maggie set before him, which appeared to contain a mixed-up blob of ingredients.

Maggie grinned. "Karla calls it Heavenly Hawaiian Surprise. It's got pineapple and cherries and pecans and marshmallow and sour cream, and trust me, it is heavenly."

"We shall see, or better yet taste," Mitch said, his teasing eyes alight with affection.

His brother beat him to it. Scooping up a spoonful of the mixture, he popped it in his mouth.

"Decadent," he pronounced. "Delicious."

Once again Justin's low, ultrasensual tones sent an unfamiliar, unwanted and unappreciated chill down Hannah's already quivering spine. At the same time, the spark in his eyes caused a strange melting heat deep inside her.

Hannah resented the sensation but, to her chagrin, she felt every bit as attracted to Justin as she was wary of him. All he had to do was look at her to make her, in a word, sizzle.

Dammit.

It had been some time since Hannah had warmed to a man and she had certainly never sizzled for one. But innate honesty compelled her to admit to herself that she did indeed sizzle for Justin.

And she didn't like it at all.

The conversation around the small table was general; for Hannah, desultory. Appearing for all the world comfortable and relaxed, inside she felt stiff, frozen solid.

Later that night, after the brothers had finally left, Hannah lay awake in the surprisingly comfortable roll-away bed Maggie had prepared for her. She examined the conflicting emotions Justin Grainger had so casually and seemingly effortlessly aroused inside her mind and body.

She felt empty, needy. It was almost frightening. How could it have happened? Hannah asked herself. She was hardly the type to become all squishy and nervy from the mere expression in a man's eyes and the low, sensual sound of his voice.

Certainly, Justin had not said or done anything out of line. He had been every bit as polite and respectful as had his brother Mitch.

Except for his eyes. Dear heavens, Justin Grainger's sharp and compelling eyes.

A shiver trickled through Hannah, and she drew the down comforter more closely around her. She knew it wasn't the coldness of the air but an inner, deeper chill that wouldn't be banished by burrowing under three down comforters.

Hannah decided that getting through the next days—the rehearsal, the dinner, the wedding and reception ought to prove more than a little interesting. In fact, she was afraid it would be an endurance test.

Was she up to the sort of sensual challenge those glinting, gray eyes promised?

Hannah believed she was. She was her own woman, which was why she had struck out on her own, preferring to work her tail off to establish herself rather than work for somebody else.

There was just one tiny flaw in all this—while Hannah *believed* she could handle the situation, return home unscathed by Justin Grainger, she wasn't absolutely certain.

And *that* was frightening.

* * *

"So what did you think of her?" Mitch asked as he and Justin settled into his car after leaving the large house.

Her? Justin hesitated. "Who?"

Mitch glanced over to give Justin an are-you-kidding? look. "Maggie, who else. You remember—the woman I'm going to be marrying in just a few days."

"Well, of course I remember," Justin retorted, feeling like an idiot and not liking the feeling. 'But if you'll recall, there were two women in the apartment," he said in his own defense. "Although I did notice you had eyes only for Maggie."

Tossing him a grin, Mitch flicked on the motor. "I do recall that there were two, smart-ass," he chided. "I also recall that you seemed to stare at Hannah a lot."

Justin shrugged in what he hoped was a care-free way. "Hey, she's an attractive woman."

"Yes, she is," Mitch agreed. "But, that doesn't answer my question. What did you think of Maggie, your future sister-in-law?"

"She is both beautiful and nice, as you well know," Justin answered, relieved to have the topic back on Maggie and off Hannah. "And she is most obviously head-over-heels in love with you. Although I can't imagine why."

"Because I'm sexy as hell?"

Justin gave him a droll look. "Since when?"

"Since I was fifteen," Mitch shot back, as he shot out of the parking lot at the rear of the house. "Of course," he qualified, "I was following your bad example."

"Hmm. Bad example, huh?" he drawled. "Personally, I never considered it bad to be sexy."

After returning to the hotel, Justin closed his room door behind him and leaned back against it. He inhaled deeply and released the breath on a soft "Whew."

Old fashioned? Prim? Proper? Virginal? And probably plain? Had he really held such a preconceived opinion of who Hannah would turn out to be?

"Hah." Shaking his head as though he had just taken a blow to the temple and was still groggy in the mind, Justin pushed away from the door muttering to himself.

"Hannah Deturk is the most cool, composed, beautiful, long-legged woman this ol' son's weary eyes ever landed on."

He chuckled. "And you, Justin Grainger are talking to yourself."

Well, at least he wasn't cursing, Justin consoled himself, releasing a half groan. He was surprised at his unexpected emotional, and physical, reaction to the blond goddess.

Sure, it had been a while since he'd been with a woman, but not nearly long enough to explain the immediate surge of lust he'd experienced at first glance. He'd felt like a teenager in the throes of a testosterone rush.

In that instant Justin decided he had to have Hannah Deturk, in every way possible. Either that or he just might expire from the mind-blowing need.

The tricky part was; how and when? Well, he knew exactly how, Justin mused, a smile twitching the corners of his mouth. But the trick was when. Time was limited.

There were only a few days to go until the wedding. As Maggie and Hannah hadn't seen each other for six months, they'd likely be spending most of those days—and nights—together, chattering away.

Poor Mitch was going to be sleeping alone from now until his wedding night. He'd probably be a bear until then, working overtime to conceal his feelings.

Then Justin realized something—Mitch wouldn't be the only man working to control strong urges.

Damnation.

He mulled over the problem of private time and place with Hannah as he sat on the edge of the bed and pulled off his best pair of boots. Standing to shuck out of his clothes, he folded them neatly before sliding them into the plastic laundry bag provided by the hotel. His mother had been a real stickler about neatness.

Naked as a newborn, he stretched his length between the chilled sheets, doused the bedside light and started up at the ceiling. Of course, he really couldn't see the ceiling, as the closed drapes shut out even the tiniest glimmer of moonlight and the room was as dark as pure nothingness.

It didn't matter to Justin, because he could still see a shimmering image of Hannah Deturk.

"Oh, hell," he muttered, his breathing growing shallow as his body grew hard. "Think, man. When are you going to have the chance to approach her?"

The days leading up to the big event were out. There was the rehearsal late in the afternoon the day before the wedding, to be followed by the re-hearsal dinner. That night was out, as well. Justin knew full well his family would make a lengthy celebration of the dinner.

Naturally, the actual day of the wedding was out.

The day—or night—after the wedding? Justin mulled over the problem, allowing his body to cool down a few degrees. He was in no hurry to get back to the ranch, he could spare a few days for fun and games.

Not in a hotel room. Justin gave a sharp shake of his head against the pillow. Not with Hannah. He didn't want to delve into why it mattered. It never bothered him before where he spent time romping with a woman—a hotel room, motel room, her apartment, it made no difference to him. This time, if there were to be a time with Hannah, it did matter.

So then, if not the hotel, where?

He could probably have the use of Mitch's apartment, seeing as how he and Maggie were off the day after the wedding to one of those island re-sorts exclusively for couples.

No, that wouldn't do. Mitch's apartment was on the top floor of the casino, and there was no way

Justin would escort Hannah either through the front entrance of the casino or up the back stairs.

Without knowing how he knew, Justin felt Hannah was definitely not a back stairs kind of woman. Scratch Mitch's place. The same for Maggie's attic hide-away. He felt positive that Hannah would not for a second even consider her friend's home for what he had in mind.

Suddenly he was struck by a memory. There was an apartment two floors below Maggie's place. Karla had lived there before marrying Ben. It hadn't been rented since then. So they would have privacy for their baby, Ben and Karla were staying in it now. They were planning to leave the morning after the wedding, as well.

Perfect. All he had to do was inform his brother of his intention to stay in the apartment for a couple of days after the wedding. It would be empty. Besides, the house belonged to the family, and he was a member, wasn't he?

The best part was he had already laid the groundwork by telling Mitch he would be looking for female company while he was in town.

Suddenly Justin laughed aloud. Damned if he wasn't planning a seduction. Hell, he had never in his life made plans to actually seduce a woman.

He had simply homed in on a female who appealed to him, made his move and, if the woman was willing, let it all happen.

His laughter faded as fast as it had erupted. Of course, everything depended on when Hannah was planning to return to Philadelphia and, more important, if she would be willing to spend some mutually entertaining time with him.

Of course, Hannah hadn't appeared overwhelmed by his masculine appeal. Come to think of it, she had barely spoken or looked at him during dinner. But he had a feeling something shimmered between them from the moment he touched her hand. And damned if he wasn't going to give it his best shot.

"So, I understand our family's going to go off in separate directions right after the big day," said Justin who was seated at a small table in Mitch's office the following morning. He'd called his brother and invited himself for breakfast. They had finished their meal, and Justin sat back in his chair, sipping at a mug of steaming coffee.

"Far as I know, everybody's taking off about the

same time," Mitch replied from opposite Justin, his hands cradling a matching mug. "Aren't they?"

"I'm not." Justin took another sip. "Ben can take care of things at the ranch, so I think I'll lug my gear over to the apartment Ben and Karla are presently occupying and camp there for a couple days."

"Why?" Mitch raised his eyebrows.

Justin gave him a slow, suggestive grin. "I do recall telling you I'd be on the lookout for some female companionship, didn't I?"

Mitch grinned back. "You're incorrigible."

"Not at all," Justin denied. "I'm just hot to trot, is all. You don't mind if I use the place for a while?"

"Why should I mind?" Mitch shrugged. "The house belongs as much to you as it does to me." He gave Justin a wry look. "As long as you wait until everybody has left to track down a playmate."

"Everybody?" Before Mitch could respond, he went on, digging for information. "Just the family, or does that include other guests?"

"Other guests?" Mitch frowned. "What other guests? Since Maggie's parents decided not to fly in from Hawaii after we informed them we'd stop by on the way to our honeymoon, the only other guests are employees and a few local residents."

"And Hannah." Justin kept his voice free of inflection, other than a slight hint of disinterest.

"Oh, yeah, Hannah." Mitch pursed his lips. "Hmm…you know, I don't have a clue as to her plans. Maggie hasn't said a word. I'll have to ask her."

"Is it important?" Justin had to focus to retain his near-bored tone. "I mean, does Hannah come under your no-shock edict?"

Mitch pondered the question for a few seconds, then said, "I haven't given it a thought. Does it matter?"

"Only if it's going to cramp my style. Such as it is."

Mitch shook his head. "I wasn't aware that you had a style. I thought you just jumped the first woman that appealed to you."

"Only if she's willing."

Mitch raised his eyes, as if seeking help from above. "You are not to be believed." His lips twitched. "My very own brother, a philanderer, of all things."

"Hey," Justin objected. "I am not a philanderer. I'm a normal male, with a healthy sexual appetite. And do you have any idea how long it's been since I've appeased it?"

Mitch let rip a deep, rich laugh. "I don't think I want to know anything about your sex life, thank you."

"Sex life? Who the hell has a sex life?" Justin chuckled. "I talk to horses most of the time, and most of the time I don't mind. But, every now and again, a man needs a woman. And in my case, buddy, it's been months."

"Okay. Okay." Mitch held his hand up in surrender. "I give up. Have your R and R, but try not to lose the ranch at the tables downstairs."

Justin didn't bother to respond. Mitch knew damn well he wasn't stupid; he would set a limit, a fairly low one, and stick to it. He hid an inner smile. "If things break my way, I'll be too busy with more important—and a helluva lot more interesting—things than gambling."

Three

Friday arrived much too soon to suit Hannah. Although they talked almost nonstop, there hadn't been nearly enough time for her and Maggie to catch up with each other's lives. Not once had either one of them run out of things to say.

The rehearsal was scheduled for five in the small church just a few blocks from the big Victorian house. Dinner would be at the Bullock Hotel immediately following the rehearsal.

By four o'clock Maggie was a nervous wreck.

"All this over a rehearsal?" Hannah said, trying

hard to contain a laugh. "I can't wait until tomorrow. You'll probably be a basket case. Instead of walking in front of you, Karla and I might have to walk behind, in case you collapse on the way down the aisle."

"Not at all," Maggie said, giving a dainty but superior sniff. "Don't forget, I'll have Mitch's brother Adam to walk me down the aisle." She no sooner had the words out, when she burst out laughing. "And believe me, friend, Adam's big enough to handle delicate little ol' me."

"Shall we be off?" Hannah asked.

"I suppose we'd better," Maggie agreed.

Giggling like two teenagers, they clattered down the stairs and out of the building to Hannah's rented SUV.

The streets had been cleared of snow and the short jaunt to the church took only minutes. That parking lot, also cleared, already contained several vehicles.

"It looks like we're the last to arrive," Maggie said, her voice quavery with tension.

"Yes, it does," Hannah agreed, tossing her friend an exasperated look. "And will you calm down, for pity's sake? It is only the rehearsal."

"I know…but…"

"No buts." She pushed open the door. "Let's go and get this show on the road, so we can get to dinner." She grinned at Maggie, hoping to ease her nerves. "I'm starving."

The rehearsal went off without a hitch…for everyone except Hannah. She was fine at the beginning. Maggie introduced her to more of Mitch's family including his brother Adam. Hannah had immediately liked him.

Adam was just as tall and handsome as his brothers, a little older, but pleasant and charming. His eyes, unlike Justin's, were warm, friendly. So she was feeling good, relaxed, until she began leading the procession. The sight of Justin, standing beside Mitch at the end of the aisle, had the strangest effect on her.

In direct contrast to Mitch, who was wearing a dark suit, white shirt and striped tie, Justin was dressed in a soft brown pullover sweater, tan casual pants and the same black boots he'd worn at Maggie's that first night.

Hannah couldn't help but wonder if he were planning to wear the boots for the wedding. The errant thought flittered through her mind that at least the boots were shined.

But his footwear or clothes weren't the cause

of her weird reaction. It was his eyes, his laser-sharp eyes. After slowly raking the length of her body, they seemed to bore right through her, to her every thought, every emotion. And Hannah's range of emotions were running wild, shaking up every particle of her being.

She suddenly felt nervy, excited and vaguely frightened, chilled and hot all over, as if in anticipation of something earth-shattering about to happen.

Weird hardly described it.

It seemed to take forever for her to traverse the relatively short aisle, and yet she reached the end way too soon. And there he was, his piercing gray gaze glittering with a sometime-soon promise of that anticipated, dreaded, earth-shattering event. The heat causing the glitter left little doubt in her mind what he intended that event to be.

Hannah's breathing was labored, uneven. Relief rushed through her when she stepped to the side, out of his direct line of vision. Hannah rigidly avoided his eyes through the rest of the proceedings.

After that, everything went off without a hitch…until they arrived at the hotel.

Dinner itself was fine. The food served was ex-

cellent, Mitch's family friendly, easy to talk to…
that is, except Justin. He had waited until Hannah
was seated, then, deliberately, she felt certain,
seated himself directly opposite her. At once he
proceeded to renew sending his silent, visual messages to her. Hard as she tried—and she gave it her
best shot—Hannah couldn't misinterpret his intent.

She was not without experience in the nuances
of eye conduct and body language. He had plans,
for her and him together, those silent messages
promised. And, as she had suspected in the church,
every one of those plans were sexual in nature.

While Justin's hot-eyed gaze revealed his car-
nal thoughts to Hannah, his occasional and brief
comments were bland, almost banal.

Hannah didn't know whether to be amused or
run for her life.

She attempted to assure herself her feelings
were caused by revulsion, but she knew she was
lying. The truth, which she would fiercely deny if
questioned, was that her feelings stemmed from
excitement.

Hannah was fearful her feelings, the heat
steadily building inside, were clearly revealed on
her face, in her eyes. She hoped the picture she

presented to the company, even the most keen of observers, was that of cool, controlled composure.

Especially to Justin.

Justin could read Hannah like an open book. Far from being repelled by his stare of unconcealed desire, Hannah was receptive, her own needs and desires revealed in the depths of her so-cool eyes.

He couldn't wait to get her alone, feel her mouth yielding to his kiss, her naked body sliding against his, her long legs curling around his waist.

Stop it, Justin ordered his wayward thoughts. Damned if he wasn't getting hard, right there under the table. He drew a mental image of himself, trudging across the frozen tundra, chilled to the bone.

Moments later he was surprised by the strains of music from a group positioned in front of a small dance floor at the end of the private dining room. Leave it to Mitch to have arranged for dancing after dinner.

In a flash, Justin was on his feet, circling the table to Hannah. "I suppose we're expected to rehearse the wedding party reception dance, too," he said, holding out his hand in invitation.

"Ahh…" she responded, her voice laced with uncertainty and a strong hint of reluctance.

"That's right," Maggie said, laughing—bless her heart. "We want everything perfect."

Hannah sighed, but complied, placing her hand in his as she rose from her chair.

Justin's own heart was starting to speed up as he led Hannah to the dance floor. While he wouldn't be able to feel her satiny skin sliding against him, or her tempting mouth pressed to his, or the embrace of her slender legs, he was determined to feel the thrill of her supple body held close to his in the dance.

Not exactly the dance Justin would have preferred, but it would have to do…for now.

Fortunately, the group was playing his kind of music, a ballad, allowing for only slow dancing. At the edge of the dance floor, Justin drew Hannah to him, circling her waist with his arms, leaving her little choice but to circle his neck with her own. The sensation created by the feel of her tall body held closely against his was thrilling beyond anything he had ever felt while fully clothed.

Scratch that last thought, he corrected himself, drawing in a quick breath at the sensations sent skittering through him at the touch of her hand sliding from the back of his neck to the center of his chest. Though he knew her movement was intended to keep some distance between them, Justin was forced to suppress an involuntary shiver at the scorching feel of her palm against him, right through his shirt.

"What are you afraid of?" he asked, his voice pitched low for her ears only. "You don't like dancing?"

Hannah lifted her head to gaze at him, a wry curve on her maddeningly tempting lips. "Not particularly," she drawled. "And I don't need my suit pressed, thank you."

He laughed, refraining himself from telling her he intended to press a lot more than her clothes. He held himself in check for one reason; he had heard the slight breathy catch in her voice underlying her dry tones.

Deciding to play it cool, he made a half step back, feeling a chill, even from that tiny span between them.

"I'm glad you find me so amusing," she said, keeping her hand solidly pressed to his chest.

"Oh, I find you a lot more than amusing," he said, fighting an urge to be explicit, and a bigger urge to show her, right there on the dance floor.

But no, the room was full of people, most of whom were family members. If he gave in to the urge, Mitch and Adam would be all over him like a bad rash in no time. He'd hate like hell to have to deck the two of them in front of the family. The thought made him smile.

Hannah felt…bedazzled. Where the heck had that almost boyish, impish smile come from? she wondered, feeling an unfamiliar warmth around her heart. What in the world was Justin thinking about to cause that smile?

"You look pensive," he murmured, trying to move her closer to him, relenting when she resisted.

Having lowered his head, his breath tickled her ear, all the way to the base of her spinal cord. Two conflicting thoughts tangled together in her bemused mind—wanting this dance to end soon and hoping it would go on forever.

Throwing caution aside, she decided to be candid. "I was just wondering where that smile came from…and who it was for."

He laughed. Damn, Hannah wished he wouldn't do that. His laughter had an even more intense effect than his smile. It was low, infectious, relaxed, and scattered the warmth in her chest, setting off minisparklers throughout her body.

Now he grinned. She swallowed a groan.

"Actually, I was thinking about having to take down both of my brothers in front of everybody here."

Startled by his reply, Hannah stared at him. "But…why would you think of such a thing?"

His eyes gleamed with devilment. "In self-defense, of course. Why else?"

The music stopped. She made a move. He didn't. His hold was unbreakable. She swept a quick look around to see if anyone was watching them. There were three other couples on the floor: his parents, Mitch and Maggie, and Ben and Karla. The three couples were too absorbed in one another to pay any attention to her and Justin. Still, Hannah had just opened her mouth to protest, when the music started again. He moved, taking her with him, and they continued dancing.

Hannah sighed, heavily so he couldn't possibly miss it, but she had to ask, "Why on earth would you need to defend yourself from your brothers?"

"Because they'd jump me for sure," Justin responded patiently, as if the answer should be obvious.

Hannah didn't know whether to hit him or scream at him. She did neither. She sighed again and narrowed her eyes. "Okay, if you want to play games. Why would they jump you?"

"Because I want to play games," he explained, the gleam in the depth of his so cool eyes literally dancing.

"Justin…" Her voice held a gravelly, distinct note of warning.

"Okay. But don't say you didn't ask." He shrugged. "I figured if I acted on impulse, pulling you tightly against me and ravishing your mouth with mine, Mitch and Adam might think it was their duty to rescue you from the clutches of their womanizing brother." Laughter skirted on the edges of his serious tone. "And in that case, of course, I'd have little recourse but to sweep out this barn with them."

Sweep out this barn? Barn? Hannah sent a quick glance around the well-appointed dining room. But she didn't question his remark. Her attention had focused on one word. "Womanizing?"

Justin nodded solemnly, immediately ruining the effect of his somber expression with another one of those breath-stealing smiles.

She stopped moving so suddenly his big body crashed hard into hers, knocking the breath out of her. Reflexively he tightened his arms around her, steadying her while keeping them both upright, her body crushed to his.

"Nice," he murmured, his breath ruffling the tiny hairs at her temple…and her senses.

"You're a womanizer?" she blurted without thinking, her voice betraying her shock.

"No, sweetheart," he denied, his tone adamant, thrilling her with the casually stated endearment, his lips setting off a thrill as they skimmed a trial from her ear to the corner of her mouth.

"But, you said…" she began, stirring—not struggling—to put some small distance between them. Her puny efforts proved unsuccessful.

"I know what I said." His arms tightened even more. "Stay still. You feel so good." His mouth took a slow, erotic journey over her surprised, parted lips. "You taste so good. I could make a feast of you."

Because she suddenly craved a deeper taste of him, she felt a faint curl of panic. Afraid of the strange sensations churning inside her, Hannah turned and pulled her head back, away from his tantalizing mouth.

"You've got the wrong woman," she said, somehow managing to infuse a thread of strength into her breathy voice.

"No." Justin shook his head, but loosened his hold, allowing her to move back a half step. "I've got the right woman." His smile and eyes were soft, almost tender. "Hannah, I am not a womanizer."

She frowned. "Then why did you say you were?"

"Because my brothers tease me about my lifestyle every time we're together." He grinned. "Matter of fact, Mitch called me a philanderer just the other day." He heaved a deep sigh. "It was unkind of him. I was crushed."

"Right," Hannah drawled, raising an eyebrow in disbelief. "I know it's none of my business, but…" she hesitated. It most certainly was her business: Justin Grainger had definite and obvious designs on her.

"But?" he prompted, a dark brow mirroring hers.

"What is your lifestyle…exactly."

"Pretty damn boring," he said, releasing her when the music stopped. "I ranch, and I don't go to town, any town or city, too often."

"Have you ever been married?" she asked.

"I was. I've been divorced now for almost five year," he said, his voice hard and flat. "And no,

I don't want to talk about it. I want to forget about it."

Feeling rebuffed, Hannah's spine stiffened. "I don't recall asking you to talk about it...or to dance in the first place as far as that goes. Now, if you'll excuse me?" She didn't wait for an answer but strode away, head held high.

A little while later—though it seemed like hours to Hannah—the party began to break up. At last, she thought, rising and scooping up her handbag. After not having exchanged one word with Justin since returning to the table, she not only didn't say good-night, she avoided eye contact with him.

Feeling a need to escape the room, and Justin, she found Maggie, who was lingering over saying her farewells to the others, and murmured her intention of getting the car.

Hannah saw the snow flurries a moment before she reached the hotel exit. Fortunately, only a fine coating of white covered the parking lot. She didn't notice the thin layer of black ice beneath the snow as she stepped outside.

She took only three steps before she felt the heel of her right boot begin to slip. Hannah tried to regain her balance, but knew for certain she was going down.

"Son of a…" she began, her arms flailing.

"Whoa," Justin said from right behind her, his strong hands grasping her upper arms to catch her, ease her upright. "Is that any way for a lady to talk?" His hands moved, swinging her around to face him.

"I wasn't feeling much like a lady at that moment," Hannah said, still catching her breath from the near tumble, and not the nearness of the man, she assured herself.

"I can understand your reaction. That was a close one." Though it would seem impossible, his voice contained both concern and amusement. "Good thing I was only a few steps behind you."

"Thank you," Hannah said, a bit shakily, forcing herself to look directly into his eyes.

"You're welcome." His smile was a tormenting tease, his eyes held that gleam again.

He was close, too close. She could smell the clean, spicy, masculine scent of him, feel the warmth of him through her winter coat. "Were you following me?" She attempted a step back; he drew her closer.

"Yes." His lips brushed her ear, his warm breath tickling the interior.

A thrill shimmered the length of her spine; Hannah told herself it was the chill in the air, the feel of the cold fluffy snowflakes kissing her cheeks. "Why were you following me? What do you want from me?" Stupid question, as if she didn't already know the answer. Nevertheless, when it came, so blunt, so determined, she was shocked…and a lot more than thrilled. She felt allover warm and excited.

"Long, hot nights on smooth, cool sheets."

Four

At last the wedding day arrived. The candlelight ceremony was scheduled for six, with the reception following immediately at the hotel.

To Hannah's amazement, after the nervous fits Maggie had suffered the day before, her friend had been calm and remained so throughout the day.

Although she revealed not the slightest hint of it, Hannah felt like the basket case she had expected Maggie to be. Of course, her inner jitters had nothing whatever to do with her encounter with Justin in the parking lot, she kept telling herself.

Yeah. Right.

So stunned had she been by Justin's blatant suggestion—suggestion, heck, it was an outright declaration of intent—Hannah retained only a vague memory of him, chuckling softly as he walked her to her car. And, darn it, how had he been so surefooted, when he'd been wearing heeled boots, too?

"Time to dress," Maggie happily announced, ending Hannah's brooding introspection.

At last. At last. Hannah smiled, nodding her agreement. She was of two minds about the coming hours; relieved at finally getting it over with, and filled with conflicting amounts of trepidation and anticipation, more of the latter than the former.

Calling herself all kinds of a ditz didn't do a thing to calm down her seesawing emotions.

One thing was for certain. Hannah was determined there would be no slipping on black ice. At her advice, both she and Maggie wore low-heeled winter boots and carried their fancy wedding shoes in shoe bags. At least they didn't have any concerns about holding up their dresses out of the slushy mess, as both garments were cocktail length. Maggie's dress was a simple and elegant, long-sleeved white velvet, with a nipped-in waist and full skirt. She looked both innocent and gorgeous.

Hannah's dress was as simple and elegant—a sheath with three-quarter-length sleeves and a modest neckline.

They arrived at the church with five minutes to spare until show time. Apparently everyone else, including the groom, was already in place. Karla and Adam were waiting in the small foyer. Adam took their coats, and Karla handed them their bouquets. Maggie's was made of white orchids. Hannah's bouquet was the same as Karla's, a mix of dark-red rosebuds with lacy ferns and delicate white baby's breath.

Now Hannah knew why Maggie had insisted she hunt down a dress in forest green. Hers was only a shade darker than Karla's.

Music from the organ filled the church.

Flashing Maggie an encouraging smile, Karla stepped out, heading down the aisle. Offering her own smile to the bride, while drawing a calming breath for herself, Hannah followed two steps behind Karla.

And there he was, standing beside Mitch, looking devastating in a white shirt, somber tie and dark suit that was fitted perfectly to his wide-shouldered, narrow-waisted, long-legged body.

As she drew nearer, Hannah lowered her gaze, fully expecting to find black slant-heeled boots. Surprise, surprise. Justin was actually shod in classic black men's dress shoes.

When she raised her eyes, her gaze collided with his smoldering stare.

Good grief! The man was a menace. Hannah felt hot. She felt cold. She felt exhilarated. She felt exhausted. In short, she felt like a woman fiercely physically attracted to a man. A man who didn't so much as attempt to hide his intention from her.

Unaware of the ceremony going on about her, she automatically received Maggie's bouquet.

Her heart pounding, her pulse racing, finding it increasingly difficult to think straight, Hannah almost completely missed the exchange of vows.

"With this ring, I thee wed."

The firm, clear sound of Mitch's voice broke through Hannah's mental fog. She blinked, and just caught the movement of Justin handing Mitch a plain gold ring.

Her cue. Releasing a soft sigh of relief for coming to her senses in time, Hannah slipped a larger matching gold band from her thumb, just as Maggie repeated the vow.

Moments later Mitch kissed Maggie, to the applause of the guests, and it was over. They were married.

Hopefully, till death did them part, Hannah thought, frowning as she saw Justin take Adam's place in line, leaving his older brother to escort Karla.

What was the devil up to now? Steeling herself, she took Justin's arm to follow the newlyweds down the aisle to the church foyer.

"Your place or mine?" Justin murmured, his eyes glittering with a positively wicked gleam of amusement.

He knew. Damn the man, he knew exactly how she was feeling, *what* she was feeling, as if the word *ready* had magically appeared branded on her forehead in capital letters.

"I don't have a place here," Hannah muttered, riveting her gaze on the back of Maggie's head. "My place is hundreds of miles from here, in Pennsylvania."

He chuckled.

Hannah cringed, covering it with a tight smile as she hugged first Maggie, then Mitch, wishing them good luck before turning to stand beside Mitch to form the greeting line. Not daring to so much as glance into Justin's eyes again, she stood stiff, staring directly ahead. It didn't do her a bit of good, as he continued to torment her in that low, deep, nerve-rattling sexy voice.

"My permanent place is not as far away. In Montana," he murmured, his head so close to hers she felt his warm breath caress her ear. "But I have a temporary place here, as I know you do. Conveniently, both places are at the very same location, that beautiful old Victorian house."

Hannah was genuinely shocked. "Maggie's apartment? I...I couldn't, wouldn't dream of it!" she softly protested, suddenly realizing she had not said no to *him*, but rather to meeting him at Maggie's adorable little flat on the third floor.

"Of course not," he agreed, drawing her startled gaze just as he smiled at Karla who settled in line next to him. His eyes still gleamed with a sinful light. "But I haven't the least hesitation in using the roomier apartment on the first floor for some fun and games."

Fun and games. The overused expression, following the tired line of your place or mine, didn't sound as worn-out and dated coming from Justin's sensuous mouth. Truth be told, the soft invitation sounded much too tempting.

At a loss for a coherent retort, Hannah felt a wave of relief as she turned her head to find the first of the guests, Justin's parents, who were laughing and crying and hugging Maggie and Mitch in turn.

Justin merely lowered his head closer to her, his whispered words tickling her inner ear and every nerve ending in her body. "I'll be moving in for a couple of days tomorrow, right after Karla and Ben vacate."

Hannah had to suppress a visible tremor as his tongue swiftly speared into her ear.

"Feel free to visit at anytime…day or night," he murmured, increasing the tremor a hundredfold. "Come early…and often—" he chuckled at her quick, indrawn breath, "—and stay late…like a couple of days."

Thank goodness, at that moment Justin's father swept her into a celebratory embrace, as she found it difficult to pull a comeback from her mush of gray matter. The man was nearly as tall as his three sons, but not as strong as them, and not nearly as ruggedly handsome as Justin—darn his too-attractive hide.

His mother, a lovely woman, and almost as tall as Hannah took her hands and leaned forward to kiss her cheek. "You look beautiful in that dress, Hannah," she said, delicately dabbing at her eyes with a tissue. "Both of you do, you and Karla."

"Why, thank you," Hannah responded, lowering her head to kiss the older woman's still smooth cheek. She had liked Mrs. Grainger from their first meeting. "Maggie picked the color. She insisted I search until I found the perfect dress."

"And you did. It's a perfect color for so soon after the holidays," the older woman said, smiling as she stepped into Justin's waiting arms. "It's lovely on you."

Wrong on both counts, Mom, Justin thought as he swept his mother into a hug and planted a kiss on her cheek. That dark green was great against Hannah's blond hair and creamy complexion any time of year. And she didn't look merely lovely, she looked ravishing. And as for it being lovely on her, he'd rather see it off her. And he intended to…soon.

Naturally, Justin didn't say any of that to his mother. She just might have decided to step in and protect the lovely Hannah from her "bad boy" son.

He complimented her instead. "As always, you not only look wonderful, Mother, you smell terrific, kinda sexy. I'll bet Dad loves that scent."

"Justin Grainger!" His mother sounded shocked, but she couldn't quite control the amusement twitching the corners of her lips. "Behave yourself."

"He doesn't have a clue how to do that," his father drawled, the glimmer in his eyes similar to the light dancing in his son's. "But, you know what?" he said, drawing his wife from Justin's loose hold. "He's exactly right. I do think that perfume's sexy. It turns me on."

His mother gasped and proceeded to scold her grinning husband. Justin thrilled to the soft sound of laughter from the woman by his side. He smiled at Hannah.

"They're a trip, aren't they?"

"I think they're perfect together." Her returned smile caused sudden heat and potentially embarrassing sensations in all parts of his body.

"I think we'll be perfect together, too."

"To quote a wise woman I recently met, 'Behave yourself, Justin,' before you embarrass me," she said sternly, giving him a brief, pointed look at one particular part of his anatomy, "As well as yourself."

He laughed aloud, he couldn't help it. This gorgeous woman thoroughly delighted him.

Hannah simply shook her head in despair of him and turned her attention to the line of waiting guests. Then she ignored him until the last couple of guests had finally departed.

Thinking her advice prudent, at least until he got her on the dance floor at the reception, Justin conducted himself like the perfect gentleman throughout the boring ordeal of being prodded and pushed into position by the fussy photographer during the snapping of the wedding pictures.

While he drew impatient with his self-imposed restraint, and at the seemingly endless procedures, he still was distracted and amused by the quick, suspicious glances Hannah winged his way every so often.

Although he felt at the point of busting loose, Justin maintained his circumspect demeanor during the time-honored rituals of the start of the reception. He didn't even suggest that Adam again change partners with him as the wedding party made their entrance.

Toasts were raised, seemingly never-ending toasts. As best man, Justin gave the first one, and even managed to deliver it without firing one risqué shot at Mitch. Adam stood up after him, and followed his lead of propriety. It was their father, the unrepentant, rugged seventy-five-year-old zing-tosser that scored with a couple of sly innuendoes.

Braving their mother's startled and annoyed expression, Justin joined his brothers and the guests in laughter. He was happy to notice that Maggie, Karla, his sisters and even the tempting Hannah were laughing.

Within seconds, at a teasing, endearing smile from his father, his mother gave in to laughter, too.

It set the mood for the celebratory party. Growing impatient to hold Hannah in his arms, Justin remained stoic throughout the rest of the preliminaries.

There was dinner. A buffet fairly groaning with the weight of the food. Servers stood behind the long table, slicing roast beef, baked ham and roasted turkey. Then there was an array of all kinds of hot vegetables, salads and fruits.

Would this never end? Justin wondered, filling his plate then only picking at the food. Not anytime soon, he concluded, hearing the announcement for the bride and groom's first dance.

The first dance ended and the frontman for the small band called for the attendants to take the floor. Schooling himself, Justin swept Hannah into his arms and onto the floor, keeping a respectful distance between them.

She gave him a wary look, as if recalling the way he had held her the night before.

Justin offered her a polite smile. "Did you enjoy your dinner?" he asked, his tone every bit as polite as his smile. "I noticed you didn't take very much to eat."

Hannah still looked wary. "I really wasn't hungry."

"I suppose you didn't notice, but I wasn't, either." He smiled at Adam and Karla as they danced past. "At least, I wasn't hungry for food."

"Justin." Her voice was soft, stern. Her gaze narrowed on his. "Are you going to start up again?"

"Oh, honey, I've barely begun." He grinned. "May I see you back to the house?"

Her eyes glittering defiance, she raised her chin. He was tempted to take a tasty bite of it.

"No. Thank you." She gave him a superior, mocking smile. "I have my own car."

Releasing her hand, Justin took a half step back,

feigning shock. "You mean, my brother didn't send a limo for his prospective bride and her attendant?"

"Of course not. Why should he? I rented a large SUV. And he did have the limo to bring them here from the church."

"Even so, I'd have sent a limo for my intended." His eyes refuted his self-righteous tone. Reclaiming her hand, he whirled her around.

"And do you have an intended hidden away somewhere?" She was slightly breathless from his sudden quick movement. A becoming color bloomed in her cheeks.

Justin was intrigued, wondering if his swirling action had caused her pink breathlessness, or if it had sprung from her question. "No." He gave a fast and sharp shake of his head. "No intendeds for me." He lifted a dark, chiding eyebrow. "If there were, I wouldn't be here, now, wanting to make love with you."

She made a sound that to him was part gasp, part sigh. He waited for a response from her, feeling breathless himself.

At that moment the music ended, and she slipped out of his arms and damned near ran to the bridal party table.

* * *

For someone who was usually calm and collected, Hannah was feeling more than a little rattled. Rattled, excited and annoyed.

No intendeds for me.

What was he trying to tell her with his emphatic statement, the quick negative shake of his head? He had no use for women? Hannah gave a silent but definite "Ha!" Justin obviously had one use for women.

Just then, Maggie found her. "Hannah, I want you to come with me." Her friend grasped her arm, tugging to get her moving.

Trailing along, thoroughly confused by the urgency in Maggie's voice, Hannah asked, "Where are we going…and why such a hurry?"

"We're going up to the suite Mitch reserved for us for tonight," Maggie explained—kind of—continuing to tug on Hannah's arm.

"I don't understand." Now she was more than confused.

"Of course you don't." Maggie exhaled as the doors to the elevator slid together after they stepped inside. "I want you to help me out of my dress."

"Me?" Hannah could only stare at her in disbelief. "Maggie, isn't that Mitch's job?"

"Yes, yes, I know all that." Maggie waved the question aside. "But Mitch is the one who asked me to give you another heads-up." The doors swished open, and Maggie swished into the corridor. "Besides," she added over her shoulder, "I would like you to take my dress back to the house for me."

"I'd be happy to take it with me." Tired of trailing in her friend's wake, Hannah strode forward to walk with her to the suite. "Heads-up about what?" she asked, with wide-eyed innocence, as if she didn't know damn well it would concern Justin somehow.

"Justin." Maggie unlocked then flung open the door and ushered her inside.

Who would ever have guessed? Hannah thought, resigned to hearing more negative tidbits about Justin's character, or lack of same. She sighed, might as well get it over with. "What about Justin?"

"Well…" Now, after having given Hannah the bum's rush from the reception room, Maggie hesitated.

"He's a wanted felon?" Hannah asked, facetiously.

"No, of course not." Maggie tossed an impatient look at her. "Apparently, he's something of a…uh…philanderer. You know, the no-strings, love-'em-and-leave-'em type."

Big shocker. Hannah had figured that one out for herself. If she hadn't, she wouldn't have been about to bid good-night to Maggie and Mitch, wish them happiness, give them both a congratulatory hug and head for the nearest exit.

"I suspected as much," Hannah said, with self-imposed equanimity, walking around Maggie to unhook and pull the waist-length zipper on her dress.

"You did?" Maggie swung around to face her. "How?"

Hannah actually contrived a reasonable-sounding chuckle. "Dearest friend, Justin has been making…shall I say…explicit suggestions to me since the rehearsal supper last night."

"Aha," Maggie crowed. "Mitch was right. He said he thought Justin was hitting on you. That's why he asked me to clue you in."

"I appreciate the concern." In point of fact, even though she had figured Justin wasn't looking for a real relationship, Hannah wasn't at all sure she did appreciate the concern, or the information. She gave a frowning Maggie a serene smile. "Where is your bridegroom, by the way?"

"Oh my gosh," Maggie yelped. "He'll be here any minute. If you don't mind," she said, stepping out of the dress, "I'm going to toss this into the bag and toss you out of here so I can get ready for him."

Laughing with genuine amusement, Hannah retrieved the long, heavy plastic dress bag and held it open while Maggie slipped it onto a padded hanger and beneath the garment bag.

"Okay, I'm outta here."

"Wait," Maggie ordered, stopping Hannah as she turned toward the door. Bending to a low table, she scooped up her bouquet and shoved it into Hannah's free hand.

"What are you doing?" Hannah demanded. "You're supposed to toss that to the single women downstairs." She tried to hand it back to Maggie, who refused to take it.

"What single woman?" Maggie backed away. "As far as I'm concerned, *you* are the only single woman here…which means, you'll be the next bride."

"But, Maggie, you know there is no—"

"I know, I know, but who knows what's in the future? Mr. Right might be just around the corner." Laughing at Hannah's skeptical expression, Maggie backed up another step. "Will you just take it and get out of here?"

Hannah heaved an exaggerated sigh. "Okay, you win. But only because I don't want to be here to cramp his style when Mitch arrives."

"Thanks, love," Maggie fervently said, rushing to Hannah to give her a hug. "For everything, especially being my friend. I'll call you after Mitch and I get back."

"I'll be waiting," Hannah said, holding the bag up from the floor as she moved to the door. "Be happy." She smiled, opened the door, then turned back to murmur, "Love you."

Maggie's return smile was misty. "Back at you."

Five

Avoiding Justin as she made her escape, Hannah didn't breathe fully until she locked the door behind her in Maggie's cozy attic flat.

Nervous, edgy, both afraid—and secretly hopeful—that she'd hear Justin rap at the door any second, she carefully hung Maggie's dress away before removing her own dress. After a quick shower, Hannah slipped into her nightshirt and robe, then proceeded to collect her stuff. She was leaving, going back to Philly, first thing in the morning.

She was *not* running from Justin, Hannah kept telling herself, knowing all the while she was lying. She knew, without a shred of doubt, Justin would not force any issues or hurt her in any way. Why she was convinced he would honor her decision, whatever that might be, she didn't know, but she felt certain she was right.

So, if she was not running from fear of Justin, what was she running from? She was attracted to Justin, fiercely attracted. She had never, ever wanted a man, his touch, his kiss, his possession as much as she wanted Justin Grainger.

It scared the hell out of her.

He scared the hell out of her.

Not physically. Emotionally.

As sure as Hannah was that Justin would never physically harm her, she was equally sure he could devastate her emotionally.

She had been warned. Justin himself had told her he was the family "bad boy," and to protect her, Mitch had instructed Maggie to inform her of his brother's love-'em-and-leave-'em reputation with women.

Perhaps, Mitch had had a heart-to-heart with his wayward brother because, by 2 a.m. he had neither rapped on the door nor rung Maggie's phone.

Hannah knew the exact time, because by 2 a.m., she had not slept, had not so much as closed her eyes. Her restless, wakeful state had nothing to do with not having heard from him, she assured herself. She absolutely did not feel let down, disappointed…damn near bereft.

Sigh. She had done a lot of sighing.

Somewhere around 4 a.m., well, actually, 4:14 to be exact, Hannah faced the cold hard fact that Justin had been amusing himself by teasing her, stringing her along. For all she knew, he simply might have been deliberately coming on to her to rile his brother Mitch.

If that had been Justin's aim, he had scored a direct hit. Problem for Hannah was his barb had scored a direct hit on her, as well.

Her own fault. She had walked fully conscious into the cross-hairs. Served her right if she was feeling the sting of his arrow. She deserved the piercing stab in her chest. She had known full well that his make on her was all about sex, anyway.

So, the hell with Justin Grainger. She'd forget him in no time once she was back in Philly, back to her real life of work and friends.

But first she had to get some rest. She had a lot

of driving in the morning to get to the airport in time for her flight. Sleep, stupid, Hannah scathingly told herself. Clenching her body against the aching emptiness inside, she shut her eyes tight, denying the sting burning her eyelids, and concentrated on the word sleep.

Her alarm went off at seven, approximately one hour and twenty minutes after she had finally drifted off.

Groaning, Hannah levered herself off the cot and stumbled into the bathroom. Even though she had showered last night, to get an early start this morning, she pulled off her nightshirt and stepped under a spray of tepid, wake-up water.

It helped, but not a helluva lot. Heaving a deep sigh, followed by a wide yawn, she brushed her teeth, applied a layer of concealer on the dark half-moons beneath her eyes, and finished with a light application of tinted moisturizer and blush to each cheek.

Frowning at her image in the mirror above the sink, Hannah left the bathroom, made up the cot. Deciding to grab something to eat in the terminal concourse, she skipped breakfast for a fast get-away. Quickly dressing, she stomped into foul-weather boots, pulled on her coat, gathered her baggage and sent a final glance around the cozy flat, checking that everything was in order.

Swallowing another sigh, which she adamantly refused to admit was of regret, Hannah left the apartment and clattered down the stairs to the second-floor doorway. Yanking open the door, she stepped into the hallway and practically into the arms of Justin Grainger.

"What kept you?" he said, a lopsided smile on his smooth, clean-shaved face.

Startled, rattled, Hannah stared at him. "Wh– what?"

"I thought you'd never get it together this morning." His warm gaze caressed her face, settled on her mouth. "I heard your alarm go off all the way down two flights of stairs—what the hell have you got, anyway, a miniature Big Ben?" Before she could open her suddenly tingling lips to reply, he caught her by one arm to lead her along the hall to the other stairs. "I hope you didn't waste time eating. I've been holding breakfast for you."

"But...but..." Hannah stammered. Dammit, she never stammered. "Why?" she demanded, allowing him to relieve her of her suitcase and carry-on with the other hand as he urged her down the stairs and to the open door of the apartment where Karla and Ben were staying.

"Why not?" he asked, ushering her inside and firmly closing the door behind them.

More unsettled than she would have believed a man, any man could make her, Hannah ignored his question to ask one of her own. "Where are Karla, Ben and the baby?"

"They left before daylight. I helped them load the SUV. They're going to visit her folks in Rapid City before heading back to the ranch," he explained.

"So, why were you holding breakfast for me?" But before he could respond, she went on, "And how did you know I'd agree to have breakfast with you?"

Justin held up one finger. "I thought you might be hungry." He grinned—too darned sexily—and held up another finger. "I didn't know. I hoped. Will you?"

He had done it again. Thrown her off track. "Will I…" she blurted, before she collected her senses. Never in her adult life had a man held the power to so fluster her.

"Share a meal with me." His grin turned into a sensual smile; his lowered voice was sheer temptation. "Among other even more satisfying pleasures."

"I, uh…" Damned if she wasn't stammering again. Grabbing a quick breath, she stammered, "I…really…I don't…uh…think that…would be wise," she finished, all in a breathless gush.

"Maybe so," he drawled, in that same low, tempting tone. "But it would be fulfilling …for all our hungers."

"I know." Hannah blurted out without thinking, amazed at herself for doing so. "But that's beside the—"

"No, that *is* the point," he interrupted, setting her bags aside to cradle her face in his warm palms. "I want to be with you so bad I ache all over," he murmured, lowering his mouth to within a breath of hers. "And I feel, no, I know you want to be with me every bit as badly."

"How…" Hannah swallowed. Her voice was barely there, because suddenly her throat was tight, dry. "How do you know I want what you want?"

"Ahhh, sweet Hannah," he whispered, his breath slipping between her slightly parted lips and into her mouth. "Your eyes give you away." His mouth skimmed across hers, setting off a sensation that sparkled throughout her entire being. "Admit it…" His voice gathered a wicked, teasing thread. "So we can get on with other things, beginning with breakfast, which I can smell is ready."

It wasn't until he mentioned it that Hannah caught the mouthwatering aroma of freshly brewed coffee, meat sizzling and something she couldn't quite identify, but which tantalized her taste buds.

"Okay," she said, giving in, not to him, she told herself, but the rumble of emptiness in her stomach. "I'll have breakfast with you." Chastising her weakness, she hurried on, "But then I must get moving or I'll miss my plane."

"There'll be other planes." Very softly, very gently, he touched his mouth to hers.

Hannah couldn't answer. She couldn't breathe. His half kiss had turned the sparkle inside her to tongues of flame.

She stood mute while Justin lifted the strap of her handbag from her shoulder and slid her coat from her arms. She didn't protest when he stashed her coat, handbag and two cases into a small closet. Turning back to her, he smiled, melting what felt like her fire-charred insides, and held out a long-fingered hand.

"Come…let's have breakfast."

* * *

Hannah was well and truly stuffed, pleasantly so. Cradling her second mug of coffee in her hands, she sat back in her chair, replete, one hunger satisfied.

"More?" Justin raised one dark brow, smiling at her over the rim of his coffee mug, reigniting another, even more basic hunger inside her.

"Good heavens, no." She returned his smile, if a bit shakily. "Thank you. Everything was wonderful."

"You're welcome." He lowered the mug; his lips were moist from the beverage and much too appealing. "And thank you, I'm glad you enjoyed it."

"I certainly did. Do you cook a lot?"

"Not often, I admit, but I can cook."

"A man of many talents?"

"Oh, honey, you'd be amazed."

Always before, Hannah had resented a man calling her honey, yet, somehow, coming from Justin, it didn't bother her. The fact was, she rather liked it.

"Refill?" he asked, raising his mug.

"I don't think so." She shook her head before swallowing the last of the coffee and setting her mug on the table. Hannah stood, telling herself to get moving before she gave in to the desire to stay and indulge herself. "I've got to go home."

"Why?" he asked with a grin. "I was tempted to say—Home is where the heart is—but," he shook his head. "I decided that was a bit too obvious."

Though she really tried, Hannah couldn't contain a smile. "And practically everything you've said to me, every suggestion you've made, wasn't obvious?"

He pulled a long face—an attractive long face. "And here all the time I thought I was being subtle."

She burst out laughing. "Subtle? Justin Grainger, you are about as subtle as a jackhammer."

"You deeply wound me." His words were belied by the devilish light in his eyes. He set his cup aside and started toward her. "Is that any way to being an affair?"

"Affair?" Hannah felt a thrilling jolt. "We, uh… we're not beginning an affair." She took a step back. He took two steps forward. "We hardly know each other." She held up one hand…as if she actually believed that would stop him.

Of course it didn't. Justin kept moving, slowly backing her up until her spine made contact with the kitchen wall. He raised his hands to cup her face. His palms were warm, gentle. His long fingers stroked her cheekbones.

"Justin." Hannah would have drawn a deep breath, if she could have found anything other than the most shallow wisp of air. "Don't." Her breathless voice was a mere half-hearted whisper, hardly a deterrent.

Still, Justin paused, his mouth within inches of hers. He sighed, as if held motionless by that one word don't. "Oh, sweet Hannah, don't tell me no," he murmured. "If I don't kiss you soon, I'll explode."

Hannah raised her hand to his shoulders to move him back. She felt the muscles grow taut beneath her suddenly gripping fingers. And then, amazing herself with her boldness, she slid her hands to the back of his neck, grasped his hair, and pulled his head to hers to devour his mouth.

Justin did a fantastic job of devouring in return. Holding her head still with gentle fingers, he angled his mouth over hers. His tongue outlined her lips, teased the sensitive inner skin, before exploring deeper, engaging her tongue in an erotic dance.

Hannah could barely breathe, and she didn't

care. His mouth was heaven, his tongue a seeking, probing, ravenous instrument of sensual torment.

His hands deserted her head to glide down her spine, cup her bottom, draw her to the fullness of his body. All rational thought dissolved, swept away by a torrent of sensation, part agony, part pleasure, all terribly exciting and arousing.

He could have this effect on her with one kiss? Hannah marveled, in an obscure corner of her disintegrating mind. What would making love with him do to her?

On the spot, without having to give it a moment's thought—which was good, since she couldn't think anyway—Hannah knew she had to find out, possess him while she experienced his possession of her.

"Hannah, sweet Hannah," Justin groaned into her mouth, lifting his head to stare into her pleasure-clouded eyes. "You can't kiss me like that then tell me you must leave, that we're not beginning an affair."

"I know," she admitted in a raw whisper.

Justin drew back another inch to study her expression. "You want me, don't you, sweet Hannah?"

She didn't answer at once, but stood staring

back at him. Able to breathe a little, and almost think, Hannah was struck by the realization of having lost count of the times he had called her "sweet Hannah." She had been called many things in her life, from "squirt" by her older brother, to "the cool one" by her friends, to "beautiful," even "stunning" by hopeful lovers but never "sweet." If anybody had said she was sweet, she'd have bristled, been annoyed. Babies were sweet, not mature, adult women.

So, then, why did she melt at the endearment murmured through Justin's so-tempting lips?

"Hannah?" The thin, sharp edge on his voice yanked her from her muddled reverie.

She blinked. "What?" Then she remembered his question. "Oh…yes," she answered with complete honesty. "I do want you, Justin," she confessed, spearing her fingers into his thick dark hair.

His soft laughter had a joyous ring. Releasing her bottom, Justin flung his arms out to his sides. "Then take me, sweet Hannah. I'm all yours."

Hannah accepted his invitation by pressing her mouth to his.

Without breaking contact, Justin moved Hannah away from the wall, through the small dining room and in the direction of the bedroom.

Drowning in multiple sensations, Hannah was only vaguely aware of his arms curling around her waist, holding her entire body tightly to his. But she was fully aware of heat rising inside her at the feel of his hard muscles against her softer flesh.

Entering the bedroom, Justin shut the door with a backward tap of his bare foot. Still without breaking the kiss, he carried her to the side of the bed. Setting her on her feet, he released her, stepped back and brought his hands to the hem of her sweater.

Trembling with need, Hannah raised her hands and the sweater swished over her head, landing who knew, or cared, where. She was fumbling with the buttons on his shirt when an errant but important realization stilled her fingers.

"You need to know that I'm not on any kind of birth control. I haven't used anything for over two years now."

He frowned at her statement. "That's pretty risky, isn't it?"

"Not at all." She shook her head, a bittersweet smile shadowing her lips. "I...haven't...er...indulged—" She broke off to shake her head once more. "You know."

"You haven't had sex in two years?" His voice, his startled expression, hovered somewhere between amazement and disbelief. "Are you serious?"

"Yes." She sighed.

His expression turned pained. "You don't like sex?"

She had to smile. "Well, I don't dislike it." She sighed again. "It's just that," she lifted her shoulders in a hapless shrug when his frown deepened to a near scowl. "I haven't felt attracted…that way…to a man, any man, since I ended a relationship a little more than two years ago."

"Why did you end the relationship?" he asked, in a tone that said he wasn't sure he really wanted to know.

"It was mutual," she answered. "It simply wasn't working for either of us."

"What wasn't working?" His gaze probed intently into hers. "The sex?"

"Well…yes," Hannah confessed, lowering her eyes to the allure of his half-naked chest, suddenly aware of her own near nakedness. "I owe it to you to admit that I fear I may be, uh…unresponsive." She drew a deep breath before rushing on, "I've never had an orgasm."

"You're kidding."

Tired of feeling like a feminine failure, Hannah lifted her head and boldly stared straight into his shocked eyes. "No, I am not kidding. Dammit, do you think any sane woman would kid about something so serious?"

"No, I suppose not," he agreed. Then he asked, "You said you wanted me. Did you mean it, or were you just experimenting with me?"

"I meant it." Hannah's tone was filled with conviction. "I do want you."

"Good," Justin purred, the flame of desire flaring again in his eyes. Lowering his head, he brushed a taunting kiss over her mouth. "Then let's get on with it, see if we can't give you that orgasm."

The mere brush of his mouth robbed her of breath, sent her senses whirling.

"What about…um," she said between quick breaths, "protection?"

Justin smiled. "Luckily for us," he said, shoving his hand in a jeans pocket and retrieving a foil-wrapped package, "I *do* practice safe sex."

Six

Hannah lay where Justin had placed her, right in the center of the queen-size bed and watched as he stretched his long length next to her.

"Hannah, Hannah," he murmured. "What am I gonna do with you?"

She gasped and opened her eyes in wide innocence. "You need instructions?"

Justin laughed gently. "That does it, sweetheart. Now you are really gonna get it."

"Really, really?" Hannah curled her arms around his neck to bring his mouth back to hers.

She was thoroughly enjoying herself, never before had she teased and laughed while making love. "Will I like it?"

"Let's find out," he whispered, taking command of her mouth with his.

Deepening his kiss, he slid a hand over her shoulder, down her chest to the rounded slope of her breast. Gasping, Hannah arched her back, seeking more of his exciting touch. Growling into her mouth, he cupped her breast, found the hardening peak with his fingers.

Heat flowed like molten lava from the rigid peak to the core of her femininity. Hannah was on fire. She couldn't breathe but she didn't care. She wanted more and more.

Squirming to get closer to him, she lowered her arms and pulled him tightly against her straining body. Her hands made a tactile exploration of his broad back, his narrow waist, his slim hips, his long well-muscled thighs.

She needed something…something.

"Slowly, sweetheart," he softly said, his lips following the trail laid out by his hand. "We have all day." His tongue darted out, electrifying her as it flicked that aching peak. "There's plenty of time."

That was easy for him to say, Hannah mused,

moaning deep in her throat at the exquisite sensations his tongue sent quaking through her. She was on fire, every inch of her burning for...that elusive something.

Grasping his hips, she urged him to her, arching in an attempt to align their bodies. Resisting, holding himself back a few inches from her he slid his hand down the center of her quivering body.

"Justin." Hannah cried out as his stroking hand found, delved through her mat of tight blond curls and into the very core of her.

"Justin!" she cried out again, her voice now a near sob, as he parted the delicate folds to explore the moist heat within. "I...I...please!"

"Please what, sweet Hannah?" He delved deeper as he raised his head to her mouth, spearing his tongue between her parted lips, capturing her gasping breaths.

She arched her hips into his tormenting hand, and slid her mouth from his. "I need...need..." she paused to pull some air into her lungs.

"Me?" he whispered enticingly, slipping the tip of his tongue into her ear.

"Yes, I need you, your body...now!"

"At your service, sweet Hannah." Continuing to tease her by gliding his tongue to the corners of her mouth, Justin settled himself between her thighs.

Hannah immediately embraced him with her legs, urging him closer, closer. She gave a hoarse cry when he thrust his body deeply inside her. He set a quick, hard rhythm. Holding on to him for all she was worth, she arched back her head and strove to match his deep strokes. It was a very short ride.

The fire inside her blazed out of control. Hannah felt the unbearable tension quiver, then snap.

"Justin!" Her voice was raw, strangled as her body convulsed around him. In reaction to the sheer pleasure pouring over her, and without conscious direction, her nails scored his buttocks, thrilling once more when he attained his release, growling her name, over and over.

Pure ecstasy. Hannah wanted to tell him, thank him, but at first she couldn't find the breath. Then, when her breathing evened enough to speak, before she could put the thought into words, she succumbed to the sleep that had eluded her during the long night.

"Hannah?" Getting control of his own breathing process, Justin lifted her sweat-slick head from her equally moist breast to look at her. Her eyes were closed, and she looked serene, disheveled but serene. She was breathing at a normal sleeping rate. "Knocked you clear out, did I?"

Smiling, he disengaged, lifted his depleted body from hers. Stretching out beside her, he drew her soft, pliant body to his, pillowing her cheek on his chest.

"Ahhh, Hannah, sweet Hannah," he murmured, not wanting to wake her. Well, with the swift response of his body to the satiny feel of hers, he actually did want to wake her, but he held himself in check, letting her rest.

She'll need it, he thought, rubbing his cheek against the silken, tangled mass of her hair, his body growing harder at the memory of her long blond tresses spread wildly on the pillow in the throes of passion.

And Hannah was passionate. Justin could still hear the echo of her voice pleading with him, her nails raking his skin, crying out to him in the intensity of her orgasm.

Her response had triggered the strongest, most shattering orgasm he had ever achieved, he thought, aching to repeat the experience.

Good grief, were Hannah's former lovers complete idiots? How could they not be as fired up—

roasted, in fact—as he had been to her quick, passionate sensuality?

A shot of sheer male satisfaction flashed through Justin as he realized he was the first man to bring Hannah to ultimate completion.

And ultimate was the only way to describe it. She lay thoroughly satiated and relaxed in the protective cradle of his arms, one of which was growing numb. Justin didn't care. Ignoring the sensation and the discomfort of his hard body, he closed his eyes.

"Sweet, beautiful, Hannah," he whispered, kissing the top of her head as he drifted into a light doze.

The afternoon sun rays were slanting into the room when Hannah woke. She felt good. No, she mused, yawning. She felt wonderful…but hungry. No, that wasn't quite right, either. She felt famished, in another part of her body as well as her stomach.

She made a tentative move in the confines of Justin's caging embrace, sliding her body against his.

Justin. A thrill skipped up her spine at the memory of what they'd shared. With his mouth, his hands, that strong hard body, he had given her a gift beyond her wildest imagination. Not only in her delicious release, but by freeing her fears of being frigid.

"I was beginning to think you had died."

His breath tickled her scalp, his low, intimate tone tickled her libido. "For a moment there, I think I did." Tilting back her head, she smiled up at him and nearly melted at the tender expression on his handsome face. "Isn't that what the French call it. The little death?"

"Yeah." His mouth curved invitingly, a flame springing to life in the depths of his eyes. "Wanna do it again?"

"Yes, please," she said, sliding her free hand up his chest to toy with one flat male nipple. His response was so swift it was breathtaking.

Grunting like a caveman, he heaved himself up and over her, settling her flat on her back. Precisely where she wanted to be at that moment. She opened her legs for him.

"Not so fast, sweet Hannah," he said, laughing down at her as he lowered his head to hers. "You had your way with me the last time. This time it's my turn."

She pouted at him. Still chuckling, he crushed her pouting lips with his hungry mouth.

This time the little death was even more intense; the release, mind and body shattering. Never had Hannah expected to feel as if she were soaring above the clouds. Talk about a natural high! Justin's slow, fantastic loving had brought her to the point where she had actually screamed in response to the sensations of joyous bliss.

Hannah might have been embarrassed by her uncontrollable outcry, if Justin's shout hadn't almost immediately followed her own. Still buried deeply inside her, he lay, spent and relaxed, his head pillowed on her breast. Moving beneath him, she rubbed her leg over his buttock and down the long length of his muscular thigh.

He murmured something against her breast, letting her know he was alive, if not altogether awake.

"I'm hungry," she said, sliding her fingers into his hair, combing through the sweat-dampened, long, tangled strands.

"Are you trying to kill me, woman?" he muttered, raising his head to stare at her in feigned astonishment. "I'm in my thirties, you know, not my late teens."

Hannah giggled. "I thought I felt something stir awake inside me," she lied, laughing into his teasing eyes.

"You thought wrong. It's out for the count." He grinned, rather leeringly. "It'll take a while before I'm ready to spring into action again. Do you think you can bear the wait?"

"I guess so." She sighed, then grinned back at him. "But I don't know how much longer I can bear your weight."

Justin groaned and rolled his eyes. "Give me strength. The woman's tossing puns at me now," he groused, lifting his body to roll over, sprawling next to her.

Hannah gave an exaggerated sigh of relief. "That's better." Arching her back, she stretched the stiffness out of her arms and legs. "I'm hungry."

"You said that." He grinned and looked down at the front of his body. "And I explained that—"

"For food, *man*," she taunted, getting back at him for twice calling her woman. She wrinkled her nose in distaste. "So drag your so depleted carcass off this bed and help me get something together to eat."

"Slave driver," he complained, laughing as he practically leaped from the bed. "I'm not doing another damn thing, bossy *woman* until I shower and shave." Circling the bed, he scooped her body up into his arms and headed for the door. "And you, sweet Hannah, are going into the shower with me."

Smothering yet another giggle, Hannah curled her arms around his neck and rubbed her face against his shoulder. "I've never showered with a man before," she softly confessed.

Justin stared down into her eyes. He shook his head, his expression compassionate. "You've never done a lot of fun things with a man, have you?"

"No."

"Did you enjoy your, er, first thing?" He arched his brows, then wiggled them.

Hannah laughed, feeling her cheeks grow warm. "Immensely," she admitted. Darn it. What was it about this man, anyway? She hadn't blushed since…hell, she couldn't recall ever having blushed.

"Then, trust me, sweetheart, you're going to enjoy this, too," he promised.

He was dead right. Hannah thoroughly enjoyed

every minute of the playful splashing, lathering, caressing, kissing beneath the spray of warm water. Who knew how long they would have remained there, if not for the audible grumbling sound of hunger from her stomach.

It was almost as much fun drying each other off.

Clean, but still naked as a newborn, Hannah dove back under the covers while Justin shaved. When he walked boldly naked into the bedroom, she unabashedly watched, admiring his lean, muscular and magnificent body as he stepped into briefs, jeans and pulled a cable-knit sweater over his head.

"See anything you like?" he asked, arching a dark brow over laughing gray eyes.

"Actually, I like the whole package," she readily admitted. "You're a very attractive and nice man."

"Boy, that last compliment is a relief." He heaved a deep sigh. "For a minute there, I thought you wanted me only for the pleasure of my body."

"Well," Hannah said teasingly. "There's that, too."

"Thanks. Hey, aren't you ever coming out from hiding? I thought you were hungry."

"I am. But I have no clean clothes here." She

made a face at their clothing scattered around the bed. "I'm waiting for you to be a gentleman and fetch my suitcases."

"I knew you were a slave driver," he muttered.

Justin was back in moments. He set the bags next to the bed, then stood watching her.

"Out," she ordered, flicking a hand at the door.

"But I wanna watch," Justin said, in tones similar to a petulant little boy.

"Are you some kind of voyeur?" Hannah asked, grabbing a pillow and throwing it at his head.

He ducked. The pillow missed him by inches. "No." He grinned. "But you watched me. Hell, I could feel you watching me. It was like a touch. And now I want the privilege of watching you."

"You don't have time to watch me," she countered, enjoying the banter. "I told you, I'm hungry."

"Then I suggest you get your tush in gear and get dressed." He moved back to prop himself indolently against the door frame. "Because I'm not budging."

Giving him a narrow-eyed glare that only brought a wolfish grin to his lips, Hannah flung back the covers and stood. "All right, then, dammit. Watch your fill."

Laughing softly all the while, Justin did watch, his appraising look missing nothing as she dug through the largest of the cases. Secretly thrilling to his caressing gaze, Hannah took her sweet time stepping into almost-there panties, fastened the front closure of her bra, wriggled into hip-hugging jeans and shrugged into a turtleneck sweater.

"You are one absolutely stunning woman from head to toe, sweet Hannah," he said in near reverence.

"Thank you," she whispered. Feeling her face grow warm again, this time with pleasure, she turned away, opening the other bag to search out footwear. Like him, she didn't bother with shoes, slipping into satin ballerina slippers.

In the meantime, Justin moved to open a dresser drawer, making do with a pair of heavy-duty socks to keep his big, narrow feet warm.

He held out his hand to clasp hers. "Now, let's go rustle something up for lunch—" he shot a look at the dark beyond the window "—or supper." He laughed. "Hell, for all we know, it may be a midnight snack."

"Not quite," Hannah said, letting him lead her from the room. "I looked at the clock. It's only nine-fifteen."

"Only, she says." He groaned, and fumbled for the light switch as they entered the kitchen. "We haven't eaten since early this morning. We're both ravenous…and the woman says it's *only* nine-fifteen."

Hannah laughed, at him and at herself. She must be losing her mind, she decided happily, because she not only didn't mind him calling her woman, she was beginning to like it. No doubt about it, her mind was starting to disintegrate. She masked her laughter with an exaggerated groan at the sight of the table still cluttered from their breakfast.

"Yeah," Justin agreed, propping his hands on his hips. "It's a mess. Tell you what, sweet Hannah. I'll make a deal with you."

She gave him a skeptical look. "What kind of deal?"

He frowned and shook his head in sad despair of her. "You have a suspicious mind, Ms. Deturk."

"Damned straight, Mr. Grainger," she retorted. "What deal?"

"Here's the deal. I'll get dinner, if you'll clean up the breakfast debris."

"Deal," Hannah accepted at once, fully aware

she was getting the better end of the arrangement. Crossing to the table, she went to work, while Justin went to the fridge.

"That was delicious," Hannah commended Justin, raising her wineglass in a salute. "You're a very good cook."

"Either that," Justin said, inclining his head and raising his own nearly empty glass in acknowledgement of her compliment, "or you actually were famished."

"I was," she admitted. "But that doesn't mean I'd have praised anything you set in front of me." She grinned. "I'd have eaten the meal, but I wouldn't have praised it, or your culinary skill."

"I wouldn't go so far as to call it a skill. I simply can manage to prepare a reasonably palatable meal. Now, my mother, she's a skilled cook."

"I like your mother, by the way," Hannah said. "She is a lovely woman. I admire the way she handles her husband and her overgrown sons…all three of whom I also like."

"Three?" He appeared crushed. "Just my father, Adam and Mitch? What about me? Don't you like me?"

Hannah's expression and tone went hard and serious. "If I didn't like you, Justin, do you really believe for one minute I would be here with you now?"

"No." He gave a quick shake of his head, his voice as serious as hers had been. "No, Hannah. I don't, for even a second, believe you would be here now, if you hadn't found something about me to like." The seriousness fled, and the gleam sprang back into his eyes. "What is it that appeals to you? My body? My…"

"Is fantastic," Hannah interjected, holding back a laugh. "And you use it to advantage."

Justin arched a brow but continued with what he had started to say, "My personality?"

She mirrored his dark arch with her lighter eyebrow. "I didn't know you had one."

He laughed.

Her pulse leaped and her senses freaked. How was it possible for one man's laughter to cause such exciting sensations inside her, Hannah mused, loving the feelings, yet scared of them at the same time.

"I like you," Justin offered the unsolicited opinion. "I like your gorgeous body, too."

"I kind of figured you did," she responded wryly.

"But I'd like to do a further exploration of the terrain." He grinned…more like leered. "Just to be sure."

"Uh-huh." She eyed him warily. "But that will have to wait. My plane left hours ago. I've got to phone the airline, see if I can book another flight."

"You've already missed your flight," Justin pointed out, his voice soft, persuasive. "Why can't you wait till morning to call and reschedule?"

"I, er…" She faltered at the brazen look of renewed passion in his eyes. At her hesitation, he shoved back his chair and stood.

"Come on, let's get the supper things cleared away," he said, collecting his plate and cutlery.

Rising, Hannah began to follow his example. "And after the supper things are cleared away, we'll go to the bedroom…."

"Good," he flashed a self-satisfied grin at her.

"To pick up the clothing we discarded and scattered all over the bedroom floor."

"Yeah, yeah," he muttered, not meaning one yeah.

Ten minutes later Justin found himself hanging the damp towels on the mounted wall racks in the bathroom. "You know, this could have waited till morning, as well," he called to Hannah, who was busy neatly folding their clothing.

"Yeah, yeah," she mimicked his agreement. "But you'll be thanking me tomorrow."

In truth, Justin did thank Hannah in the morning, but not for remaining resolute about picking up their stuff. He thanked her with words and caresses and deep, searing kisses for what he swore was the most fantastic night of his life.

Seven

"What about Beth?" The gleam in his eyes grew brighter. "Didn't you like her?"

It took a few minutes for Hannah to make the connection. She and Justin were in the middle of breakfast. This time he had cooked oatmeal, served with brown sugar. He was watching her, waiting for the dawn of comprehension to break over her sleep- and sex-fogged mind.

"Oh, your sister, Beth." Hannah felt like a dull wit. At least she hadn't said, "huh?" "I like her, very much. She stopped by Maggie's apartment a few days ago. We had a nice chat. Besides being warm and friendly, she's a gorgeous woman, a striking combination of your mother and father."

"Yeah, she is," Justin agreed, popping another spoonful of cereal into his mouth. After swallowing the oatmeal, he downed half the orange in his glass. "Adam's wife, Sunny, is no slouch either."

Nodding, Hannah took a ladylike sip of her juice. "She's lovely, and their daughter, Becky, is absolutely adorable. I immediately fell in love with her."

He chuckled around the last of his cereal. "She has that effect on everybody." He arched a quizzical dark eyebrow. "You like kids?"

"Very much." Finished eating, she dabbed her mouth with the paper napkin she had spread over her lap, and gave him a teasing smile. "Some of my best friends have kids."

"So," he said, getting up to fetch the coffee carafe to fill their cups. "What about you?"

Frowning, Hannah gave him a blank look. "What about me?"

"Don't dodge, sweet Hannah," he chided. "I've told you about myself. Now it's your turn."

Her mind may have been a little slow that morning—apparently a wild night of unbelievably fantastic sex had that effect on her—but it hadn't come to a complete stop. "You did no such thing," she retorted. "You quizzed me about my opinion of your family."

"Well, I sure couldn't give you my opinion of your family, since I haven't met them."

"Now who's dodging, Mr. Thinks-He's-So-Clever Grainger?" She grinned as she mimicked his one eyebrow lift.

He took a careful sip of his steaming coffee and grinned back at her. "Okay, what do you want to know…all my deep, dark secrets?"

"Do you have any?"

"No."

Hannah laughed, she couldn't help it. She just loved… Whoa, hold it. Loved? Don't go there, Hannah, she cautioned herself. Avoid that word like the plague.

"Are you really the bad boy your mother called you?" she asked. Not that she believed he'd confess to her all about his philandering ways.

"Of course not. I'm worse."

"Indeed. In what way?"

"You know," he drawled, "I don't know what you do for a living, but you should be in police interrogation."

"I'm in marketing," she said wryly. "And don't try changing the subject. It won't work. I want to hear all the lascivious details."

"Lascivious?" Justin tilted back his head and laughed. "You are really something, woman."

Woman. Again? Time to drag the knuckle-dragger into the twenty-first century. "Yes, actually, I am something. And don't call me woman. My name is Hannah."

He looked astounded. "You're not a woman? Damn, you could have fooled me. Yesterday morning and last night. Mostly last night. And I'll call you woman whenever I want to."

"Okay." Hannah pushed back her chair and stood. "I'm out of here." Turning away, she walked to the phone mounted on the kitchen wall.

"Wait a minute." His hand covered hers on the telephone receiver, holding it still.

She hadn't even heard him move.

"Hannah, sweetheart," he crooned into her ear. "I was only kidding. What are you doing?"

"Precisely what I said I was going to do today," she said. "I'm going to phone the airline to book another flight, hopefully for tonight or tomorrow morning."

"Hannah," he murmured, his voice a low, coaxing siren song. Releasing her hand to cup her shoulder, he turned her into his arms. "Don't go."

She raised her eyes and dropped her guard. His gaze was shadowed, compelling. Oh, heavens, she had to get out of there, away from him, because if she stayed with him…she could wind up being hurt. Hannah knew her thinking was right and yet. And yet…

"Hannah." Justin slowly lowered his head, to brush her mouth with his. "Don't go. Stay here, with me, for a week, or at least a few more days."

His tongue outlined her lips, and Hannah was a goner. Against her better judgment. Against everything she had believed about the folly of a rushed relationship, she knew it was too late to stop, too soon to bolt.

She wanted more of him. It was as simple and frightening as that. Surrendering more to her own needs and desires than to Justin's plea, Hannah raised her arms, curling them around his strong neck to draw his lips to her hungry mouth.

"You said you had been married."

"Hmm," said Justin.

Hannah couldn't see his face, since she lay tightly against him, her cheek resting on his chest.

Justin's angled body was curled almost protectively around her. The fingers of his one hand played with a strand of her long hair. The protective position of his long body sparked a memory of the night of the wedding reception.

After leaving Maggie in the bridal suite, Hannah had returned to the hotel lobby and gone straight to the coat-check counter. Draping the garment bag containing Maggie's gown over the counter, she exchanged her high heels for the boots she had worn earlier. Shrugging into her coat and toting the garment bag and the shoe bag, she considered slipping away, before Justin began looking for her.

She started for the lobby doors, but with a sigh, changed direction to go to the banquet hall where the reception was being held. Hannah had been brought up the old-fashioned way. Good manners dictated she say goodbye to Justin's family, thank his parents—whom she had learned had footed the bill for both the rehearsal dinner and the reception—for a lovely time at both events.

Peeking inside the hall, Hannah's determination faltered. Justin was standing next to the table, talking and laughing with his father and Adam, and looking far too tempting.

She was on the point of turning to leave when little Becky had come up to tug at his pant leg. Gazing down at her, his laughter changed to a tender smile, and instead of kneeling to talk to her, he bent down, his body curved protectively over her. With her pretty little face turned up to her uncle, Hannah saw her mouth move, saw Justin's move in reply before, with a laugh, he swept her up into his arms and headed for the edge of the crowded dance floor.

Hovering in the doorway, Hannah had watched, expecting Justin to whirl Becky around the floor. He hadn't. Setting her on her feet, he'd bowed like a proper gentleman, taken her tiny hands in his and danced her onto the floor.

For some ridiculous reason the sight of Justin, so careful and caring of his niece, had brought a lump to Hannah's throat and a hot sting to her eyes.

With a firm shake of her head, a stiffening of her spine—and her resolve—Hannah had used those few precious seconds while the music played to pay her respects to the Grainger family, then steal away from the hotel, and Justin.

Hannah was brought back to the present when a thought struck her. "Justin, do you have children of your own?"

Heaving a sigh, he rolled onto his back, spreading his arms wide in surrender. "No, Hannah." He opened his eyes to look at her, his expression somber. "Angie…my ex-wife, said she wanted to wait a little while before starting a family." His lips twisted, as if from a sour taste in his mouth. "Before the 'little while' was up, she put on her running shoes and sprinted away with another man." He made a rude, snorting noise. "Would you believe, a traveling computer-software sales rep? Pitiful, huh?"

"I'm sorry," she said in a subdued tone. "I shouldn't have pried."

"No." Justin moved his head back and forth on the mattress; the pillow had somehow wound up on the floor. The icy look in his eyes had thawed…somewhat. "It's okay, Hannah, you may ask anything that comes to mind."

"Did you—" Hannah hesitated, before taking a chance of making him angry, bringing back the frost. "Did you love her very much?"

He managed a slight smile. "We didn't know each other very well at the beginning. You could say it was a whirlwind thing. But yes, at the time, I loved her."

Despite his omitting the words *very much,* Hannah had to fight to control herself from betraying the sharp twinge of pain in her chest. "Are you still in love with her?" It would explain his love-'em-and-leave-'em attitude toward women.

"No." He stared directly into her eyes, his voice firm. "You want the truth?" he said, not waiting for a reply before continuing, "I realized I wasn't really in love with her a month after we got married."

She frowned. "But then…" She broke off in confusion.

Justin moved his shoulders in a shrug. "She was hot, and I was horny."

Hannah didn't know quite how to respond to his frank admission, so she circumvented that particular subject. "Have you ever truly been in love?"

"No," he answered with blunt candor. "Have you?"

Hannah smiled. Turnabout was fair play, she supposed. "No," she said, equally frank and candid. "But, like you, I thought I was for a time." Her smile turned into a small grin. "But unlike you, instead of a measly month, I believed that I was in love for almost a full year."

"So, what happened? That no-orgasm thing?"

Hannah felt her neck and face grow warm. This blushing was getting pretty damned annoying. Her expression must have revealed her feelings, because he grinned in a manner of sheer male hubris. She really couldn't challenge him on it, for he certainly had cured that *thing*. Many times.

"Partly," she admitted, on a sigh. "But that wasn't the major issue."

"What!" Justin exploded, jackknifing up to sit facing her. "Was he an idiot…or were you?" As before, often before, he didn't allow her time to answer. "Not the major issue? If you believed you were in love, I would think it would be the most important issue."

"Yes, I believe you would," Hannah said, her tone patient, her silent sigh sad. "Justin, there are more things to a relationship than sex, at least if there's any hope of the relationship lasting."

"Yeah, yeah," he brushed off her scold. "Compatibility, similar likes and all the rest of that jazz. But good sex is a very large component, and great sex even more so."

Yes, indeedy, Hannah thought, without a trace of humor but with a large amount of disappointment. Justin Grainger definitely was sexually motivated.

She sighed again. "Turned out, we weren't very compatible," she explained. "He was altogether career oriented. He ate, drank and slept his career, and it got worse with every move he made up the corporate ladder. There was no time for fun, friends, long, deep conversations."

"Or even the fun of longer, deeper, lovemaking," Justin interjected.

Hannah chose to ignore his opinion, then doggedly continued. "Understand, I was recently out of college and devoted to the marketing business I was getting off the ground. But I was often able to leave my business concerns in the office when I locked up for the night."

"And he couldn't do that?"

"No." She shook her head, at the same time wondering why she was bothering to explain all this to him when they obviously weren't going to be seeing each other again after she returned to Philly and he went back to breed horses in Montana. But she soldiered on, "I didn't simply quit, you know. I tried to make it work. I even learned to cook, a chore he knew I wasn't exactly crazy about."

He laughed.

She bristled. "Well, I never could understand why anyone would put so much time and effort into preparing an elaborate meal for someone to consume in fifteen minutes, leaving the cook to clean up afterward."

Justin laughed harder. "I'm sorry. I'm not ridiculing you."

Hannah glared at him. "Then what's so damn funny?"

"The fact that you've put my own feelings about the culinary art so elegantly into words." He had brought the laughter to a more acceptable grin. "If I want an elaborately concocted meal, complete with fine wine and candles on the table, I'll go to a fine restaurant and let an expert prepare it."

"My sentiments exactly," Hannah concurred, grinning back at him, not for a minute realizing that they were in the midst of the kind of deep conversation she had just complained about being missing from her previous relationship. Maybe that was because she never considered she and Justin ever would be in any kind of relationship...other than the physical one they were briefly conducting.

"So, what do you say we consign whoever-he-was to the dull life he deserves and get on with our own pursuits?" His grin slid into an invitingly sexy smile.

"Which are?" she asked, suddenly aware of

them sitting there, naked to the waist, and the thrill
of expectation dancing along her exposed spine.

"The dreaded kitchen duty first." The sexy
smile reverted back to a grin. "Then a shower." He
hesitated. "And I think it's time I stripped the bed
and tossed these sheets into the washer."

"Okay." Though she readily agreed, Hannah
was disappointed. Drat the man and his sensually
teasing ways. "I'll remake the bed."

"You're on." Springing from the bed, he scooped
up his crumpled jeans and put them on before reaching for the same sweater he'd worn the day before.

Quickly sliding from the bed, Hannah picked
up the robe he had earlier flung aside, and slipped
into it, belting it securely, while admiring the back
he turned away to gather his clothes.

Justin Grainger was a magnificent specimen,
his broad muscular back, his slender waist, the
tightness of his butt, the long muscles of his thighs
and calves. She sighed. Hell, she even thought he
had handsome feet!

Pathetic, she chastised herself. Who the devil
ever thought of a male's feet as handsome?

She did, that's who, and the realization was
pretty damn scary. Hurrying out of the room, Hannah kept telling herself what she was feeling was

simply a strong physical attraction, a very strong physical attraction. Nothing more.

Working smoothly together as they had the day before, Hannah and Justin had the kitchen clean in less than twenty minutes.

"Know what?" Justin said to her as she was rinsing out the dish cloth. "I'm hungry."

Dropping the cloth into the sink, Hannah turned to him and pointed out the obvious. "We just finished clearing away the breakfast things."

"Yeah, I know," he agreed, favoring her with that blasted devil smile. "But have you looked at the clock?"

Naturally, Hannah shot a glance at the wall. The clock read 1:44. Unbelievable. She and Justin had finished breakfast somewhere around nine. For some weird reason, knowing the time made her aware of the hollow feeling inside her. She shifted her gaze back to him.

"You know what?" She pulled his trick of forging ahead without waiting for a response. "I'm hungry, too."

He flashed his most sexy smile. "Good. Let's grab some lunch."

Within ten minutes, again working easily together, they sat down to a meal.

Where before they had cleaned up the kitchen in compatible silence, this time they chatted away about this and that, nothing earth-shattering, simply kitchen talk.

From the kitchen they returned to the bedroom to gather the dirty laundry. They had no sooner set foot inside the room when Justin placed a hand on her arm, stopping her in the process of bending to start collecting clothes.

"You know what?" he asked again, and once more going on without pause, "I think it would be a waste of that invitingly rumpled bed." He raised that brow and flashed that wicked smile. "Don't you?"

Hannah wanted to say no. She really did. But her vocal chords and tongue wouldn't cooperate, and what came out was a hushed and breathless "Yes."

Later, lying replete and boneless beside him, Hannah silently marveled at the sexual prowess of the man holding her firmly against him. She loved the feel of his warm skin against hers, his breath ruffling her hair, his hands smoothing, soothing her back with long strokes of his hand. She gave a soft, contented sigh. Could she possibly love…

Don't go there. Hannah repeated the order she had given herself once before. This was merely fun and games. A few days out of the ordinary.

Allow yourself a few more days of physical indulgence, then run for home as though your very emotional stability depended on it...for it just might.

Spurred by her introspection, Hannah rolled out of Justin's arms, off the bed and grabbed up her robe. "I'm taking a shower," she announced, making a bee-line for the bathroom.

"Hey, wait," Justin barked, coming after her.

He was too late. She flipped the lock jut as he reached for the doorknob.

"Hannah," he pleaded with a soft laugh. "Let me in."

"You've been in," Hannah dared to playfully remind him. "A lot. And I loved every minute of it," she conceded, smiling at his exaggerated groan. "Now I want to have a long shower and shampoo my hair. I'll see you in about a half hour...if you're lucky."

"A half hour?" Justin shouted. "What the hell am I going to do for a half hour?"

"I'm sure you'll figure something out." She turned the water on full force to drown out any reply he might make.

Hannah felt wonderfully clean as she stepped from the shower. She also was rather proud of herself, as she had finished five or so minutes faster than she had promised Justin.

Holding her robe around her, she entered the bedroom. The room was empty, not a half-naked, too-attractive man in sight. To her surprise, not only was the floor clear of their clothes, the bed had been stripped and remade.

The man in question continued to amaze her. Whoever thought Mr. Philanderer would turn out to be so domesticated?

Taking advantage of the moment or privacy, Hannah dug in her suitcase for a clean set of clothes. When she was dressed, she stepped into her slippers.

Feeling warmer, and relatively protected by the clothing, Hannah plugged in her blow dryer and went to work on her hair with a round brush. She was making progress, the long strands no longer dripping, when Justin breezed into the room.

"The sheets are in the washer. It'll shut off in about fifteen minutes." He went to a dresser to remove fresh clothing. "As you'll note, I remade the bed."

"And now you want applause?"

He grinned. "No, a kiss will do for a reward."

"I don't think so." She shook her head.

Up went the eyebrow. "You don't trust me?"

"Not for a heartbeat." Trying not to laugh at his sorrowful expression, she grabbed her brush. "You get your shower, while I finish drying my hair."

He heaved a deep, noisy sigh. "You're one tough lady, sweet Hannah. You know that?" Grumbling loudly, Justin strode to the bathroom.

Never in a million years would Hannah have believed she could have so much fun with a man. She had hardly even laughed with—Well forget that one. He had been much too serious and full of himself, among other things.

Giggling Hannah decided on the spot that she would stay on, perhaps until the end of the week with Justin. She felt relaxed and happy. Why not enjoy his company, the fun and laughter, if only for a few more days?

After all, once the few days were over, she'd be flying back to her real life in Philadelphia. Justin would be heading back to his ranch in Montana.

They'd probably never see each other again.

The thought was oddly depressing.

Eight

Hannah was home in her apartment in Philadelphia. It was Sunday. She had flown into the airport late the previous Friday and had been home for a week and one day.

She had yet to hear a word from Justin.

Well, what had she expected? Hannah asked herself, making a half-hearted attempt to dust the living room. They had spent five days together. Five wonderful days that had left her so relaxed, her assistant had noted it the moment she had walked into the small suite of offices Monday morning.

"You look positively glowing," Jocelyn had exclaimed. "Were you in South Dakota, or did you hide away somewhere in some exclusive spa?"

Hannah had to laugh. Actually, she felt terrific. "No spa, I promise I was in South Dakota the whole time."

Jocelyn leveled a measuring look at her. "Well, something put that sparkle in your eyes. A man?"

Hannah knew her soft sigh and satisfied smile gave her away. The warmth spreading up her throat and over her cheeks was answer enough. Damn her new propensity to blush.

"Aha!" Jocelyn crowed. "Was he handsome? Was it romantic? Was he great in bed?"

"Jocelyn, *really.*" Now Hannah's cheeks were burning. "You know I'm never going to answer such personal questions."

"Sure." Jocelyn grinned. "But I don't need a blow-by-blow—" she giggled "—pardon the pun. Your expression says it all."

Hannah blinked, startled. "It's that obvious?"

"Yes, boss. I'm sorry, but it is. You needed a break."

That was Monday. This was Sunday. Hannah was no longer amused, or glowing. She was hurting inside, and she feared the tiny lines of tension were about to make another appearance.

But then, she had known all along that their moment out of time couldn't last. What had she been secretly hoping for, that Justin would be on the very next flight east, following her back?

No, she hadn't hoped for that, even secretly.

But one phone call just to find out if she had arrived safely would have been nice, not to mention thoughtful. Had she really believed Justin was thoughtful? Hannah chided herself. Just because he helped her prepare meals, pick up their clothes that were forever flung without care to the floor, smooth the bedding that was inevitably rumpled? Because the last time they had made love there had been a sense of desperation? And because his goodbye kiss had been deep, lingering, as if he couldn't bear to stop?

Hannah knew better. At any rate she should have. They had played house, she and Justin, like little kids. Okay, not exactly like kids.

Hannah shivered at the memory. It had been fun, playing house together. It had been more than fun, it had been wonderful, an awakening of her senses and sensuality.

Tears misted her eyes. Why the hell had she

gone and done something as stupid as fall in love with him? For she *had* fallen in love with Justin, no strings for me, Justin, philanderer extraordinaire.

Not fair, Hannah, she told herself, swiping her eyes with her fingertips. He had never made any promises. He had been up-front with her, had offered her nothing more than fun and games. She had gone into the affair with her eyes open. She had no one to blame but herself for the empty feelings of pain and longing she was experiencing now.

Life does go on, Hannah assured herself, and so would she. There was no other choice. She had friends, a career, a business to run…a living room to dust.

Justin was on the prowl, roaming the house, unsettled and cranky. Karla would attest to it; she had been witness to his moodiness. She was beginning to eye him warily, as if uncertain what he might do.

It was the weather, he told himself, staring out the window at the nearly foot of snow on the ground that was growing higher in the driving blizzard. He felt trapped, that's what was bugging him, he thought, turning away from the scene.

Justin knew damn well his restlessness had nothing at all to do with the inclement weather. He had been raised in Wyoming, and had lived in Montana for almost ten years, had taken over the running of the ranch soon after he had graduated college. Snow, ice, winter and spring rains hadn't bothered him, except in regard to worrying about the horses.

But Justin knew full well that the animals were in their stable stalls; warm, fed and watered by Ben and the rest of his ranch hands.

"Can I get you something, Justin?" Karla asked, as he stalked into the kitchen.

Wondering what in hell he was doing there, Justin said the first thought that jumped to mind. "Is there any coffee in the pot?" It was a dumb question, and he knew it. There was always coffee in the pot. It wasn't always freshly made, but he had never demanded fresh, although he preferred it that way.

"Yes." Karla smiled at him as she opened a cabinet and took down a mug. "I just made it." She shook her head when he reached for the mug. "Sit down, I'll get it for you."

Not about to argue with the woman who prepared some of the best meals he had ever tasted,

Justin moved to the table, collecting a carton of milk as he went by the fridge.

The coffee was exactly as he liked it, strong, hot and freshly brewed.

"Would you like something to go with that?" she asked, carrying her own mug to the table. "Cookies, a slice of pie or coffee cake?"

Ever since Ben had brought Karla to the ranch as his bride, there were always cookies in the pantry and pie in the fridge. He liked her coffee cake best…although her apple pie was also delicious.

Justin glanced at the wall clock. It was several hours to go until suppertime. "Couple of cookies sound good. Do you have any of those oatmeal, raisin, walnut cookies?"

Karla laughed and headed for the pantry. "As those are both Ben's and your favorite, I always keep a supply on hand. I baked a double batch yesterday."

While Karla was inside the large storage room, Ben strolled into the kitchen from the ranch office, where he had been checking stock on the computer. In effect, Ben had virtually taken over the running of the ranch, leaving Justin feeling superfluous and adrift. He didn't resent Ben…how could he resent a man for doing a great job, especially when the man was next thing to a member of the family?

No, Justin didn't resent Ben. He simply felt useless.

"Where's my bride?" Ben asked, going straight to the cabinet to pour a cup of coffee for himself.

"Ran off with the milk man," Justin drawled, sipping carefully at the hot brew in his mug.

"Neat trick." Ben grinned as he strolled to the table. "As we don't even have a milk man."

Justin waved a hand in dismissal. "Minor point."

"You rang, Your Lordship?" Karla emerged from the pantry to favor her husband with a smile. "Was there something you wanted from me?"

Ben flashed a wicked grin. "Yeah, but this isn't the time or place. The boss is watching." He jerked his head at the plate she was carrying. "I'll settle for some of those cookies you've got there."

Their affectionate banter created a hollow sensation in Justin's midsection. Telling himself it had nothing to do with one Hannah Deturk and the bantering, laughter and tender moments they had shared, he attempted to fill the hollow place with cookies. His ploy didn't work.

Through the long, seemingly endless days that

followed, nothing worked. Including Justin. Leaving the majority of the ranch responsibilities to Ben, Justin brooded and prowled the house like a hungry mountain lion.

Hungry was the key word, and it had nothing to do with his stomach. How often had he reached for the phone, to place a long-distance call to Philadelphia? Justin couldn't remember, but he knew damn well why he had never actually lifted the telephone receiver.

What could he say to Hannah? I miss you, and I'm hard as hell? Yeah, he derided himself. That ought to turn any woman's mind and will to molten lava. And Hannah wasn't just any woman. Oh, no. Sweet Hannah was her own woman, a fact she had made abundantly clear to him from the beginning.

Sure, she had agreed to spend a few days of mutual pleasure with him, Justin conceded. And the pleasure had been mutual, of that he had no doubt. For a man who had not so much as stayed a full night with a woman since his marriage ended, the pleasure had been intense, teeth-clenching ecstasy. As for Hannah, well Justin felt certain that not even the most skilled of actresses could have faked the depth of her response.

Still, their shared desire, and compatibility out of bed, had not kept her from leaving when she said she would.

Without saying it aloud, she had made it abundantly clear that she had a life back east and she wasn't about to change it. Her determination to leave was unshakable. Despite his murmured plea for her to stay a while longer and the implied enticement of his last kiss, she had whispered a farewell, slid behind the wheel of her rental vehicle and driven away without looking back.

Unaware of heaving a heavy sigh, Justin stared out the window. The blizzard had long since blown itself out, but the temperature had not risen above the twenties since then. The snow remained, the unrelenting wind driving it into five-foot and higher snowbanks.

Damn, other than the inconvenience of getting back and forth from the house to the stables, Justin had never minded the snow before. What in hell was wrong with him?

"Why don't you take a vacation?" Ben's voice broke through Justin's thoughts. "Someplace where the sun's shining and the temp's in the eighties. Find yourself a woman. You're workin' on my nerves, and you're starting to worry Karla."

"I'm working on your nerves and making Karla edgy?" Justin said in a soft, tightly controlled voice to keep from snarling at the man. "Maybe you and Karla are the ones needing a sun-filled vacation."

"Not us," Ben denied. "Karla and I are happy here, sunshine or not."

Justin lifted an eyebrow. "And you think I'm not?"

"Oh, gimme a break, Justin. I've known you a long time, remember?" Ben shook his head. "In all that time I have never seen you like this, stalking about the house, staring out the window, sighing every couple minutes, not even when Angie took off with that smooth creep."

"I sigh every couple of minutes?" Justin drawled in feigned amusement, feeling a twinge of alarm and ignoring the reference to his ex, because *that* wasn't important. The strange sensation was. "I'll think about it," he said, ending the conversation by turning back to the window.

"Okay, I can take a hint," Ben said with a short laugh of resignation. "I'll mind my own business."

"I appreciate it."

Justin only vaguely heard Ben's chuckle as he left the room. Staring out, he didn't see the barren scene of winter white on the other side of the window. An image had formed in his mind, an image Hannah had drawn for him with her description of Pennsylvania. The verbal picture she had given him was of a different landscape, a vision of rolling countryside, lush and green, bathed in sparkling spring sunlight.

Blinking, he frowned, then turned and strode to his bedroom. Going to his desk he opened his personal laptop, and went onto the Net. He had some research to do.

Several hours later Justin shut down the computer and picked up the phone to call the company pilot in charge of the ranch's helicopter. After asking the pilot to pick him up at the pad a short distance from the house, he pulled a bag from the closet and dumped enough clothes into it to last him a couple of days.

Following the near ennui he had been experiencing since he had returned from Deadwood, the rush of anticipation he was feeling was invigorating.

Justin placed another call before striding briskly from his room. He had what he figured was an interesting and potentially very profitable idea he needed to discuss with his brother, Adam.

His battery recharged, Justin gave a brief explanation to Ben as he drove him to the landing pad. The chopper was already there, blades slicing through the frigid air.

"Not to worry," Ben assured him. "I'll take good care of the horses."

"I know you will." With a wave goodbye, Justin headed for the helicopter.

"By the way," Ben yelled over the roar of the spinning blades. "You look and sound like your old self again."

Near the end of the second week of February, Hannah faced up to the suspicions she had been mentally dodging for close to a week, suspicions induced by the vague feeling of queasiness she had in the morning, the slight tenderness in her breasts. Needing more proof than just symptoms, she stopped by a pharmacy on her way home from work.

The strip from the particular home pregnancy kit she had purchased turned the positive color. Not an altogether complete confirmation, Hannah knew. There had been cases where the strip results had proved wrong, but…it definitely required a visit to her doctor.

How could it have happened? Not even in their most heated, impromptu and wild love play, had Justin forgotten to use protection.

Of course, no one ever claimed the protective sheaths were infallible, Hannah mused as she studied the inside of her freezer, trying to decide what to have for dinner.

Having heated in the microwave the frozen meal she'd chosen Hannah sat in front of it, considering the options available to her should her doctor's examination prove conclusive.

Sliding the plate aside, Hannah laid her fork on the place mat and picked up the cup of green tea she had brewed for her dinner beverage, instead of her usual coffee.

Coffee. She sighed. She loved coffee, especially in the morning, all morning…several cups of coffee, regular, not decaf.

Hannah knew she would have to forgo her favorite drink if she decided to—

Oh, hell. Hannah took another sip of the tea. It wasn't bad tasting. It wasn't coffee, but actually was rather good as far as substitutes went.

That is, unless she chose an alternative. The thought set a wave of nausea roiling in her stomach. She gulped the tea in hopes of quelling the sensation.

She couldn't do it. Though she supported a woman's right to choose any of the options, Hannah knew that she really had only one option. Should the doctor confirm her pregnancy, Hannah was going to have a baby.

A baby. Visions of soft blankets and tiny booties danced through Hannah's mind. A fierce rush of protectiveness shot through her, and she slid a hand down over her flat belly.

Her child.

Justin's child.

The sudden realization was both thrilling and somewhat frightening. How to tell him?

Justin had been up-front with her from the beginning. He had wanted nothing from her except a brief physical affair. Their affair had been the most wonderful experience Hannah had ever known. Of course, she hadn't considered the possibility of falling in love with him.

Over the days they had been together, Hannah had learned a lot about Justin. Yet at times she felt she hardly knew him at all.

As a lover, she couldn't imagine anyone his equal. There were moments when his voice was so tender, his touch so gentle it brought tears to her eyes while at the same time setting her body on fire. And there were other times when his voice was raw and ragged, his touch urgent, his love-making fierce and demanding.

And Hannah had reveled in every minute of both approaches.

Then there were the periods when all they did was talk, sometimes teasingly, other times seriously.

Hannah had learned that Justin was honest to a fault. When he shared something of himself with her he was blunt and to the point. Not a bad quality to possess. She knew a woman had betrayed his trust and that he had no intention of walking that route again.

She also knew Justin liked kids. He had confessed to Hannah that he adored his niece, Becky. But Justin had never mentioned a desire for children of his own, other than to say his ex had wanted to wait a while before starting a family.

If the doctor confirmed her pregnancy, Hannah didn't know whether or not to inform Justin. After all, she reasoned, if Justin had any interest in a child of his own, he wouldn't have been so scrupulous about protection.

For all the good it had done them.

Still, he had a right to know he had fathered a

child. It was her duty, as an honest person, to let him know.

She just didn't know how to tell him.

Nine

Valentine's Day. The day for lovers. Hannah not only didn't leave work early, she worked over an hour later than usual. She even skipped lunch. Tired, only vaguely hungry, and not so much as considering a restaurant, especially on this special day for sweethearts, she went straight home.

Her heart skipped many beats as she stepped from the condo's elevator to find Justin propped languidly against her door. A bag was on the floor next to his crossed ankles.

The bag, along with the very sight of him filled

her with a flash of hope that he had come to Philadelphia because he realized that they belonged together.

Gathering her senses, and applying her common sense almost at once, Hannah told herself to play it cool until she heard from his lips the words she desperately longed to hear. How easy it would be for her to then tell him of her pregnancy suspicions.

Heaven help her, he looked…wonderful, like the horseman he was. With his Stetson, heavy wool jacket, jeans and slant-heeled boots, he looked exactly as he had the first time she'd seen him.

"Hi."

The low, intimate timbre of his voice nearly stopped her breathing completely. Damn his gorgeous hide. She had to repeat to herself her cautioning advice to play it cool.

"Hi." Hannah was amazed by the steadiness of her own voice, her ability to speak at all, as her throat was suddenly dry. "What are you doing here?" Door key at the ready, she aimed it at the key hole. No minor feat, considering the tremor shaking her fingers.

"I came to see you. Are you going to invite me in?"

"Yes, of course, come on in." Hannah walked inside with as much decorum as she could muster. "I didn't mean what were you doing here, at my apartment," she said, not sure if she was making conversation, or babbling on in response to the sudden attack of nervousness coursing through her. "I meant what are you doing here, in Philadelphia?"

"Well," he said, grinning as he shrugged out of his jacket, removed his hat, "I wanted to see you. Though that isn't the only reason I'm here, in the northeast."

Hannah's spirits soared at first, then took a nosedive, her hopes going down in flames. Still, she maintained her composure and took his jacket and hat and hung them away in the coat closet. The flight bag she set behind the nearby chair.

"I see." She tried to match his casual tone and didn't quite make it. "Well, I'm glad you stopped by," she said, dredging up a shaky smile to hide the sting of pain burning inside. "So," she held on to her smile for dear life. "Why else have you come east?"

"I'll tell you after dinner…" Justin hesitated, frowning. "You haven't had dinner, have you?"

"No," Hannah shook her head. "I worked late and didn't feel up to the crowds in the restaurants tonight."

"Oh." He nodded, then raised a dark brow. "You eat out often?"

Hannah wanted to scream at him. Didn't the man know that it was Valentine's Day? And what difference did it make to him whether or not she ate out often? This was only an afterthought visit, anyway.

"Occasionally," she answered, smothering the curse and a sigh. She gestured for him to sit down. "Would you like something to drink?" she asked, too politely, certain that if he said coffee she'd throw up.

"No, thanks." He sat down on the plush lounge chair. "I'll wait for dinner."

Did he actually expect her to cook for him? He'd wait until the cows came home, she fumed, using one of her father's favorite expressions. Hannah gave him a level stare and mirrored his eyebrow action. "I hope you realize that there will probably be long lines at all the better restaurants tonight," she said, making it perfectly clear she had no intention of providing a meal for him.

"I don't need a restaurant." His smile was knowing, making her aware he understood her unsubtle hint. "I've ordered dinner to be delivered here."

The audacity of the man. Why didn't it surprise

her? Everything inside him radiated audacity and…and…sheer male sensuality.

Stop that train of thought immediately, you dimwit, Hannah ordered herself. Stick to the subject at hand. "How did you know I'd be in town?"

"I didn't." Justin shrugged, then laughed that deep, thrilling, damnably exciting laugh that set her pulses racing. "But I figured I'd take a chance. I'll tell you all about why I'm here while we eat."

"But…" Hannah began to ask him how he had gotten past the security guard in the lobby, only to be interrupted by the buzz on the intercom from that very same man.

"There's our dinner," Justin said, moving to the intercom beside the door. "I'll take care of this. You go set the table."

You go set the table, Hannah grumbled to herself, whirling around to do as he ordered. As he ordered. Who the devil did he think he was?

Hannah had finished setting the table except for the water glasses she had retrieved from the cabinet. But she didn't know whether he wanted water with whatever it was he had ordered for dinner or if he'd prefer wine, which of course, she couldn't have. She set one glass on the table and was filling the other glass for herself from the refrigerator's water dispenser when she heard him open the door and speak to a delivery man. The distinct aroma of pizza wafted through the apartment.

To her amazement, instead of bringing on a wave of queasiness, the smell made her mouth water and her stomach rumble with hunger.

Carrying a large pizza box with one hand and a white paper bag in the other, Justin walked jauntily into the kitchen, his smile more appetizing than the smell of the food.

"Dinner is served, madam," he said, carefully sliding the box onto the table. "This," he added, holding the bag aloft, "is our dessert."

Someday, maybe, hopefully, you'll get your just dessert for being such a rogue, Hannah thought, but simply asked aloud, "What do you want to drink to go with it?"

"Beer?" he asked.

"Yes." She turned to the fridge.

"Beer with the pizza, and coffee with dessert."

Her stomach twitched in protest. Wishing he hadn't mentioned her previously favorite beverage, Hannah took a can of beer from the fridge and moved to the table to reach for the glass at his place.

"I don't need a glass," Justin said with a dismissive wave of his hand, popping the top while seating himself in the chair opposite hers. "Sit down and serve the pizza."

Starting to seriously resent his assumed right to order her around, Hannah fixed him with a fuming look. "You know, you could have served it while I was getting your beer."

"No, I couldn't," he said with a smile, indicating the box with a nod of his head. "The opening's in front of you. And in case you haven't noticed, the lid's taped shut."

Hannah couldn't decide if she wanted to laugh at his obvious teasing, or toss her glass of water at him. She did neither. Drawing the box closer, she broke the paper tape and lifted the lid.

The delicious aroma hit her first, making her almost groan with hunger. Then two other factors struck her, making her gasp in surprise. The large crust had been worked into a heart shape, and the words, Sweet Hannah, had been formed with small slices of pepperoni.

She laughed with delight. It was the strangest, most wonderful Valentine's gift she had ever received. "Wherever did you get this?" she asked.

"The pizzeria a couple of blocks down. I told the counter man what I had in mind. Turns out, he owns the place and he smacked his hand against his forehead and said, and I quote, 'Why didn't I think of that? I coulda made a bundle.' I told him to keep it in mind for next year." He grinned. "Are you ever going to serve it?"

Hannah pulled a sad face. "Must I?"

"Only if you want to eat…and don't want me to starve to death at your kitchen table."

"Well, in that case, I suppose I'd better." Laughing, if rather weakly, Hannah scooped up a slice and slid it onto his plate. "May I ask what gave you the idea in the first place?" she said, serving herself a slice.

"Hmm." Nodding, Justin murmured around the big bite he'd taken into his mouth. "I came up with the idea when I decided I wasn't in the mood to stand on line at a restaurant, at a candy store or a florist," he said after swallowing. "Hey, this is pretty good." He followed that with a swig of beer. "And I wasn't in the mood because I was tired after driving around since early this morning." He took another big bite.

Ready to bite into the slice she had served herself, Hannah paused, unable to resist asking, "Why have you been driving since early this morning…and where?"

* * *

Before responding to her questions, Justin polished off his slice and held his plate out for another. His hesitation wasn't because he was that hungry, although he was, but because he was carefully choosing the words of his explanation.

"Actually, I've been driving around for two days. I flew into Baltimore the day before yesterday." Justin couldn't miss the tightness that stiffened Hannah's spine, so he rushed on. "I picked up my rental car, checked into a hotel, then went to keep an appointment with a real estate agent."

She frowned. "Here? In Baltimore?"

"Yes. You see, I'm doing some scouting for Adam. We're thinking of investing in a horse farm here in the East, to breed Thoroughbreds. The agent found farms available in several states and set up appointments for me."

"What states? And why here in the East?" she asked, frowning.

"Maggie told me there were a lot of horse farms out here." He answered her second question first.

"Well, Maggie should know," Hannah said. "She was born in Berks County."

Justin nodded. "So she said. She suggested Virginia, Maryland and Pennsylvania." He polished off a third slice of pizza, grinning as he again held out his plate to her.

Hannah shook her head as if in disbelief of his capacity for food, but slid another slice onto his plate.

He plowed on. "I started in Virginia, where there were two possibilities. From there I drove into Maryland, where there were three. I stayed in a motel in Pennsylvania last night and got an early start this morning. I toured one in Lancaster County, another two in Bucks County, and the last one in Berks, in the Oley Valley."

"Oh, I've been there," Hannah said, patting her lips with a paper napkin. "My assistant is a dedicated antique-shop crawler. I go with her every so often, and one time she drove through the valley, to Oley Village, I guess that's what they call it. It's not very big, but charming."

"I didn't get to see the village or town, or whatever it's called. But the valley is beautiful, even in winter. And the property I looked at has definite possibilities." He arched a brow, wondering at the tiny, wistful smile that quirked her lips. "I'm ready for my coffee now."

"Of, of course, I forgot," she said, sliding her chair back and rising. "What's for dessert?" she asked, moving to the automatic coffee unit set on the countertop.

"You'll see," Justin answered, puzzling over her odd expression as she prepared the coffee. His puzzlement deepened as she filled a red enamel teakettle then put it on to boil and took a flower bedecked porcelain china teapot from the back of the stove and a box of teabags from the cabinet. She placed a couple of bags in the pot.

"You're not having coffee?" He didn't try to hide the surprise in his voice; he had firsthand knowledge of her passion for coffee…among other passions. He had to turn his mind to something more mundane when he felt his body stir in reaction to the sensual direction of his thoughts. "What's with the teapot?"

Hannah gave a careless shrug of her elegant shoulders. "I've developed a liking for green tea lately," she said, not looking at him as she concentrated on pouring the now boiling water into the teapot. "It's supposed to be very good for you, you know."

"Not for me," Justin said dryly. "I'll stick with my coffee…and beer."

"Well, here's your coffee," Hannah said, in a strangely choked voice. She set the steaming mug on the table, before going to the fridge for milk.

"Thanks," Justin said, pondering her odd behavior; Hannah had held the mug out in front of her as if she was afraid it would attack her. Weird. He took the carton of milk she handed him, and watched her as she returned to the countertop for the teapot and a mug.

"I don't understand," she said, obviously avoiding his gaze, as she carefully poured the pale tea into the mug. "Why would Adam be interested in another horse farm for the company, when you already have the ranch?"

"At the ranch, we breed and train Morgans, primarily for the rodeo circuit. And, as I already mentioned, we're thinking about branching out, breeding and training Thoroughbreds."

She took a delicate sip of her tea, grimaced, set down the mug and added sugar. "How many more farms are on your schedule to look at? Any other states?"

"No more states, no more farms," Justin said, singeing his tongue. "Damn, that's hot, I felt it burn all the way down," he added, reaching across the table for her half-full water glass. "Do you mind?" His hand hovered above the glass.

Hannah shook her head. "Help yourself."

Justin did, soothing the sting with a gulp of the

cool water. "I'm scheduled to fly out of Baltimore on the red-eye tomorrow night."

"Oh, I see. Are you flying home to Montana, or to Wyoming to report to Adam?" Hannah's expression didn't alter by even a shadow. She looked as she had the first time he met her, mildly interested but cool and composed. Detached.

Justin felt a wrenching disappointment. He knew, better than anyone, that beneath her facade of cool, composed detachment, a spark lay in wait to blaze into roaring flames of passion.

Dammit to hell! Why was she in hiding from him? For she was in hiding. He had sensed it the minute she had stepped from the elevator and had seen him by her door.

"To Wyoming to confer with Adam, then back to Montana," he said, working hard to control the anger and frustration building inside him.

"So you're driving back to Baltimore tonight...or have you booked a hotel here in the city?"

Justin couldn't read her expression, as she had raised her cup to her mouth, concealing the lower half of her face from him. But her voice was even more detached, cooler. The distant sound of it fanned the flame of his anger. What was she playing at, looking, speaking as if they were nothing more than casual acquaintances, when it had been less than a month since they had been passionate lovers?

Well, Justin decided, getting to his feet and circling the table to her, he wasn't about to play along. He had been missing her something fierce from the moment she had driven away from him in Deadwood.

Hell, he had tossed and turned every night, even dreamed about holding her, caressing her, kissing her. Damned if he was going to walk away without tasting her.

Coiling his hands around her upper arms, he drew her up, out of her chair, pulling her body against his.

"Justin…what…" Hannah began, her voice no longer cool, but surprised by his action.

"I think you know what," he murmured, sliding his arms around her to bring her to him, and lowering his head to crush her mouth with his.

He had meant it to be a forceful kiss, but the instant his lips made contact with hers, he gentled, drinking in the taste, the scent, the feel of her. It was like coming home, where he belonged.

The alien sensation rattled Justin deep inside.

After the blow Angie had delivered, he'd never believed he would feel such a way again.

Justin was on the point of lifting his head, breaking his near-desperate contact with her mouth, when Hannah curled her arms tightly around his neck and speared her fingers into his hair.

Needing to breathe, Justin raised his head just far enough to gaze into Hannah's eyes. "No, I am not driving back to Baltimore tonight, nor have I booked a room here in the city," he said between quick indrawn breaths. "I was hoping you'd let me spend the night here. With you. In your bed."

"Justin, I...I..."

Her eyes were warm, almost misty, the way they had looked every time she was aroused. Hannah wanted him, maybe almost as much as he wanted her. Justin knew it. Relieved, he silenced her with the brush of his mouth, back and forth over hers.

"Hannah," he whispered against her parted lips, into her mouth. "I'm on fire for you. Come to bed with me."

"Justin..."

He silenced her again, damn near terrified she was going to refuse. He ached, not only from the steadily growing, hardening of his body, but inside. He stifled a groan when she pulled her head back.

"Justin, wait, listen," she pleaded, her fingers tangling in his hair, hanging on as though she was afraid he'd let her go. "We haven't cleared the dinner things away—or had dessert."

He laughed, because it sounded so...Hannah. And because the exultation filling him had to escape.

He smiled and rested his forehead against hers. "It wouldn't be the first time, sweet Hannah. As we did before, many times before, we can clean it up later. And we can have the dessert for breakfast."

"Dessert for breakfast?" She pretended shock.

Laughing softly, Justin began an exploration of the fine, satiny skin of her face with his lips. "What I brought will do fine for breakfast, or for dessert after breakfast."

Laughing with him, in a sure sign of her surrender, she tickled his ear with the tip of her tongue. "I have never heard of dessert for breakfast."

Justin's body nearly exploded at the moist glide of her tongue into his ear. "Errr...Hannah," he said in a rough croak, "You'd better lead me to your bedroom before I lose control and take you right here and now."

"As if," she retorted, grinning as she pulled away from him, grabbed his hand and started through the living room to a short hallway. "You've never lost control."

"There's always a first time, sweetheart," he said, raising her hand to his mouth to press his lips to her fingers. "And I'd sure hate to embarrass myself in front of you."

Entering her bedroom, Hannah turned her head to give him a wry glance. "That…or are you possibly afraid your loss of control would give me a sense of womanly power?"

"Oh, sweet Hannah, you have no worries in that department," Justin said, shutting the door behind him and twirling her around into a tight embrace, letting her feel her power in his hard body. "You've got womanly power to spare."

Minutes later, their clothing tossed in all directions of the room, Hannah lay naked, eager, in the center of the queen-size bed that had felt so large, cold and empty for weeks. Also naked, Justin stood next to the bed, tall and proud and magnificent, his turbulent gray eyes watching her as she watched him sheathe himself in delicate protection.

The image would haunt her after he was gone. She knew it, would pay for it, but for now, Hannah could think of nothing except having him beside her, inside her, loving her…if only for this one more night.

She held her arms up to him in invitation. He came to her, stretching his long body next to her own. His mouth hot on hers, his hands implements of exquisite torture.

He couldn't wait, and with a murmur of need he slid his body over hers, settling between the thighs she parted for him. She couldn't wait, either. Wrapping her long legs around his waist, she raised her hips in a silent plea.

Justin's possession of her was fast and hard, exactly as she needed it to be. Their zenith was reached in shuddering, spectacular unison. Though Hannah wouldn't have believed it possible, the climax was more intense, more thrilling than any previous one she had experienced with him.

She loved him, loved him with every living cell within her, as she would love his child, their child, after Justin was gone. For then, weeping silently,

Hannah decided she would never again be a receptacle for his convenience. She just couldn't bear to be one of the women "the bad boy" visited every so often.

Holding him to her, inside her utterly satisfied body, Hannah drifted into the deepest sleep she had known since leaving him in Deadwood.

Ten

Hannah woke up at her usual time. A creature of habit, she needed no alarm. She was still tired. She really hadn't slept very much. She ached, but pleasantly so. Twice more during the night, she and Justin had made love.

It had been wonderful. No, it had been more than wonderful. It had been heavenly. Between periods of short naps and long, slow indulgences of each other, they never found time to venture out of the bedroom to clear away the dinner clutter.

Yawning, Hannah pushed back the covers Justin had haphazardly drawn over them after their last romp, and moved to get up. A long arm snaked out to curl around waist, anchoring her to his side.

"Let me up, Justin," she said, trying to pull back. "I still have to clear the kitchen table, eat something and get ready to go to work."

His arm held firm, and he rested his cheek on the top of her head. "Take the day off." His voice was low. "Stay with me until I have to leave for Baltimore."

Hannah was tempted. Lord was she tempted. But mindful of the vow she had made to herself after their first frantic bout of sex—for that's all it had been, at least for him, she reminded herself—she steeled herself against his alluring suggestion. "I can't." She shook her head and pushed his arm away. "I can't leave my assistant on her own today."

"Why not?" His sleepy voice threatened to undermine her resistance. "You did when you went to Deadwood."

Taking advantage of the momentary easing of his hold, she slipped out from under his arm. "I know, but then I had laid out all the upcoming projects, explained my ideas in detail. There are things pending that need my personal attention."

While speaking, she had collected her clothes as she made her way to the connecting bathroom.

"Hannah, wait." Justin jumped from the bed, attractive as sin in his nakedness. He reached for her.

Dodging his hand, she stepped into the bathroom, locking the door before calling out to him, "You can have the shower when I'm done." She turned on the water full blast to drown out the sound of his muttered curses.

Exhausting every curse word he knew, Justin stood stock-still next to the bed, staring at the locked bathroom door. Hannah was closing him out, exactly as she had tried to do last evening. Frustration, anger and an emotion too similar to fear to be acknowledged burned inside him.

He didn't get it. He just didn't get it...or her. One minute she was cool and remote, the next sensual and hungry for him. During the night Hannah had freely displayed how badly she wanted him, again and again.

So what happened between the last time they made love and this morning? And, dammit, they *had* made love, not merely had sex, whether or not she wanted to admit it, either to him or herself.

Shaking his head in bewilderment, he moved

around the room picking up his clothes. They'd have to talk about it, about their relationship, for, like it or not, that's what it was shaping up to be, not a one-night stand, not a slam-bam-thank-you-ma'am, but an honest to God relationship.

It scared the hell out of him. Nevertheless, an in-depth discussion was definitely called for here. He would have to make another stab at convincing her to take the day off.

Hannah had never showered and dressed so fast in her life. Her hair still damp, she twirled it all into a loose twist at the back of her head and anchored it with a few well-placed hairpins. Sighing in longing and regret for what might have been, she turned with steadfast determination and went to the kitchen. Justin stood by the kitchen table, and with a nod she indicated that the shower was all his.

She had the table cleared and wiped, dishes stacked in the dishwasher, the coffee brewing, the tea steeping, bacon sizzling and eggs whipped, ready to pour into a warming frying pan by the time Justin walked into the room.

"We forgot to say good morning." His soft voice crept across the kitchen to slither up her spine.

Gritting her teeth against a shiver, Hannah returned his greeting. "You're just in time," she said with calm detachment, dumping the egg mixture into the pan. "If you want to help, you can set the table." Without turning to look at him, she dropped four slices of bread into the toaster. She jumped when he plucked the spatula from her hand.

"I'll do the eggs," he said, his voice and his body too close for her comfort. "Since you know where everything is, it's better if you set the table."

"Okay." Hannah was glad to escape, if only to the wall cabinet a few feet from him. After setting two places at the table, she went to the fridge for orange juice and milk. "Do you want jam for your toast?"

"Do you have peanut butter?"

"Yes," she said, surprised that he also liked the spread on his morning toast.

"Natural or sweetened? I don't like the sweetened stuff."

"Neither do I," she said, removing the jar from the fridge.

Other than the odd remark here and there about the food, they ate in silence, each into their own thoughts. Feeling edgy, Hannah saw him raise a brow when she glanced at the clock for the third time. But he didn't comment on it…until after he had his coffee and she her tea.

"I think you should take the day off," Justin said, his voice laced with determination.

"I already told you I wouldn't do that," she retorted, her voice equally determined.

"We need to talk." Now his eyes were cold as gray ice.

Getting up, Hannah carried her barely touched tea to the sink, dumped it and rinsed it before replying. "No we don't. I need to leave for work." She walked from the room to the coat closet. "And you need to drive to Baltimore." She pulled on her coat and grabbed her purse.

"Dammit, Hannah," Justin said, his tone bordering on a shout. "Listen to me." He reached out to take her arm, to prevent her from walking out the door she'd opened.

Her nerves and emotions raw, her mind screaming at her to get away before she succumbed to agreeing to be one of his now-and-then women, Hannah avoided his hand as she spun around to confront him. "I won't listen to you, Justin." She was hurting, and wanting to hurt him back, if that was possible, she lashed out at him. "I have to thank you for giving me so much please," she said sarcastically. "But it's over now. You belong in Montana, and I belong here. Whether or not Adam sends you back here, I don't want to see you again."

"Hannah, you don't meant that." He sounded genuinely shocked. "You can't mean it."

"I do mean it," she insisted, fighting tears and a desire to punch him...hard, for hurting her so much. "I've got to go now." She backed out through the doorway. "I'd appreciate it if you would lock the door as you leave." With that last parting shot, she slammed the door on his stunned face.

Justin was mad. He was more than mad, he was furious. He just couldn't decide who he was more furious with, Hannah for cutting him dead, or himself for getting too deeply involved with her in the first place.

Dammit, who needed her, anyway? Certainly not him. The last thing he needed was a haughty, overly independent woman. Hell, there were plenty of warm, eager and willing women out there.

Justin repeated the assurance to himself all the way back to Montana and throughout the following three weeks. He repeated it to himself while he was working, when conferring about the horse farm in Pennsylvania they had decided to invest in, but mostly when he prowled the house at night, unable to sleep for thinking about her, aching for Hannah.

Why the hell had he been so stupid as to fall in love with her? Why had he allowed himself to fall for the Hannah that was not always cold and haughty, but sweet and hot, a tiger in his arms.

Justin knew when he was beaten. To his amazement it didn't even bother him that he'd finally fallen in love—real love. He decided he'd have to do something about it, something more than he had originally planned on back in February.

Going to the phone, Justin placed a call to Adam, his fingers tapping an impatient drumbeat as he waited for his brother to come on the line.

"What's up?" Adam said.

"We need a family meeting about this horse farm in Oley, Pennsylvania."

"Wait a minute, we've already bought the property," Adam said. "And it was your idea to begin with. Don't tell me you changed your mind and want us to back out of the deal when we're just days away from settling it."

"No, no, I haven't changed my mind about the property," Justin reassured him, "only about who we send east to manage the farm."

"Not Ben?" Adam sounded shocked.

"Not Ben," Justin concurred. "I know for a fact that Ben really doesn't want to relocate and that Karla doesn't want to move so far from her family."

"Then who the hell do you have in mind?" Adam demanded. "One of the men on the ranch?" Before Justin could get a word in, Adam added, "Is there another one of the men capable of running a Thoroughbred farm?"

"Yeah. One," Justin drawled, thinking the answer should be obvious to Adam, of all people.

"Who?" Adam snapped impatiently.

"Yours truly, brother mine," Justin said, grinning when he heard Adam sigh.

"I'll call a meeting," Adam said. "Of course, Beth will send her proxy, as usual."

Justin was now chuckling. "To me, as usual."

"Goodbye, Justin." Adam hung up.

Justin laughed out loud, inwardly praying for success in the East Coast endeavor. Not with the farm—Justin felt confident he could succeed with that. Hell, without conceit he knew he was nearly a damn genius when it came to horses. No, the challenge was convincing Hannah that he was the man for her. His plan had to work; he'd make it work…somehow.

It was the middle of March. The days were growing milder. Instead of taking the bus as she usually did, Hannah had begun walking the two-plus miles back and forth from her apartment to her office. The exercise and fresh air were good for her.

Without conscious thought, Hannah's hand slid down in a protective gesture over the small rounded mound of her growing belly. Her pregnancy had been confirmed by her doctor. Her due date was in mid-October; another season, another life.

A thrill shot through Hannah at the thought of the tiny person awakening inside her body. She hadn't felt any movement from her baby yet, but she knew it would not be long before she did.

Hannah had told Jocelyn the day after she had seen the doctor. Over a month ago.

"Does the father know?" her assistant asked, her expression a mixture of stunned delight.

"No," Hannah admitted, shaking her head. "I don't think he'd want to know."

"Not want to know?" Jocelyn said indignantly. "What kind of a user is the son—"

"Jocelyn," Hannah interrupted her, unwilling to hear her curse Justin. "I knew what I was getting into. What Justin and I had was just a fling." She managed a wry smile. "One might say a close encounter of the sexual kind. He never asked for anything more and I expect nothing from him. This is my baby. I'll take care of it."

"And I'll be right beside you," Jocelyn said staunchly, giving Hannah a reassuring hug.

Although Hannah had taken full responsibility for her pregnancy, she still had nagging doubts about not telling Justin. Not to seek financial support for his child—she didn't need his money. She just felt that he had every right to know he was to become a father.

Justin loved children. He would make a good father…if he cared to do so. That was the dilemma Hannah was feeling.

Arriving home refreshed from the brisk walk, Hannah kicked off her shoes and went straight to the phone. She had to tell him, she'd never be able to live with herself if she didn't.

After getting his ranch's number from information, she punched it in and forced herself to breathe normally. It was difficult, especially with the phone continuing to ring. Finally, when she was about ready to hang up, an unfamiliar voice answered.

"Yes, is Justin there, please?" she asked, wondering why Karla hadn't answered.

"No, he isn't," came the brisk reply. "Would you like to leave a message?"

Declining the offer, Hannah pressed the disconnect button, then stood staring at the instrument in her hand, unsure what to do next. Blinking against a sting of tears, she hung up the phone just as the doorbell rang.

Doorbell? Her doorbell never rang without her being notified by the security guard in the lobby.

Hannah hesitated, puzzled by the oddness of the situation. The bell rang again.

Hannah went into the living room and looked through the peephole. She went absolutely still.

Justin.

The bell rang once more, quick, sharp, as if punched by an impatient or angry person.

Drawing a deep, steadying breath, Hannah disengaged the lock and pulled the door open. She backed up as he aggressively stepped forward.

"Justin…" She had to swallow to moisten her bone-dry throat. "What are you doing here?"

Dropping the same bag he had carried before,

he walked right up to her and caught her face in his hands, holding her still.

"Dammit, woman," Justin said, his voice rough. "I love you, that's what I'm doing here. I didn't want to love you. I didn't want to love any woman, ever again. But I do love you." His voice softened to a gentle purr. "Oh, sweet Hannah, I love you. I want to marry you." His stormy gray eyes grew bright with that heart-melting devil light. "And if you don't say you love me, too, want to marry me, live with me and have my babies, I'm going to curl into a ball of misery on the floor and cry for a week."

"Only a measly week?" Hannah was already crying, and laughing.

"Well, maybe two," he conceded, lowering his head to hers. "But I'd rather not. Hannah, sweetheart, say it. Say you love me before I go completely crazy."

"I love you. I love you. I love you." Tears poured down her face. "Oh, Justin, I love you so much I could die from it."

"Don't you dare. We've got a lot of living and loving before us. And there's no better time than now to get started."

Holding her tightly to him—as if he'd never let her go—he kissed her, deeply, lovingly, reverently.

Pure joy bursting inside her, Hannah flung her arms around his neck and kissed him back with all the love and longing she had tried so hard to reject. She moaned in soft protest when Justin lifted his mouth from hers.

"We'll get back to that in a minute," he murmured, gliding his tongue over her lower lip in silent promise. "But I have to ask you something."

Hannah reluctantly opened her eyes. "What?"

"Will…you…marry…me?" Justin asked.

"Oh." Hannah felt a tingle do a tango down her spine. "Well, yes, of course. Was there any doubt?"

"Oh, boy," he groaned, in feigned dismay. "I have a feeling I'm in for trouble with you."

"Yes, you are," Hannah replied happily. "And I with you, but…won't it be fun?" She pulled slightly away before saying, "I said I'd marry you, Justin, and I will. But there is one possible problem."

He arched a brow. "Like…what?"

"Like…you run a ranch in Montana," she said. "And I run a business in Philadelphia."

He shook his head. "No problem."

"But…" she began in protest, afraid he'd ask her to give up the business she had worked so hard to get up and running, and even more afraid she'd agree to do so.

"Honey, let me explain," he interjected. "When I was here a few weeks ago, I didn't just stop in to visit you for a quick bout of sex at the end of my business trip."

"You didn't? Tell me more. Spill your guts, Grainger."

He laughed. "You're something else, sweetheart, you know that?"

"Yeah, yeah." Hannah flicked a hand at him. "Get on with the explanation."

"The idea of our company buying a horse farm in the East wasn't Adam's, it was mine."

"Really?" She frowned. "Is that important?"

"I think so." Justin smiled, pulling her over to the sofa where they both sat. "At my suggestion, the company bought the farm in the Oley Valley. We made settlement yesterday." He paused.

"Go on." Having an inkling of what was coming, she held her breath.

"I'm going to manage it."

"Oh...oh," she cried, almost afraid to believe it. "You're relocating?"

"Yes."

"I can keep my business? Commute?"

"Yes, sweet Hannah." His smile grew a bit shaky. "You can keep me, too, if you want."

"If? If?" Hannah exclaimed, moving into his waiting arms. "Try to get out of being kept."

Holding her tight, as if afraid to set her free, he pressed his forehead to hers. "Oh, sweet Hannah, I love you so much, so very much."

"Oh, Justin. I...I have something I must tell you, something I think is wonderful. I'm pregnant."

"You're pregnant?" Justin asked, his gray eyes starting to gleam. "You're pregnant!" He whooped, laughing. "I'm going to be a father!"

"You're not angry?" Hannah asked.

"Of course I'm not angry. I'm thrilled." He frowned. "Did you know about this when I was here before?"

She nodded. "I knew how you felt about marriage," Hannah defended herself. "I was afraid to tell you, afraid you wouldn't care or that you would think I was trying to trap you."

"Wouldn't care?" Justin appeared stunned, as though he'd taken a blow to the head.

"I...I did finally call you," she said softly, trying to placate him. "You weren't there."

"No one said I had missed a call," Justin said. "When did you call?"

Hannah wet her lips and lowered her eyes. "A couple of minutes before you rang the bell."

"A couple of—" Justin broke off, shaking his head. "You know, sweetheart, I don't know whether to kiss you senseless or shake you senseless."

"You'd better kiss me," she advised demurely. "You can't shake me in my delicate condition."

"Okay." Lowering his head, he took possession of her lips…and her heart.

* * * * *

Look for Joan Hohl's next release,
CUTTING THROUGH,
available this August
from Harlequin Next.

DYNASTIES: THE ASHTONS

**A family built on lies...
brought together by dark,
passionate secrets.**

JUST A TASTE

(Silhouette Desire #1645,
available April 2005)

by Bronwyn Jameson

When Jillian Ashton's arrogant
husband died, it wasn't long before
she found a man who treated her
right—*really* right. Problem was,
Seth—a tall, dark and handsome
hunk—was her late husband's
brother. She'd planned on just
a taste of his tender touch, but
was left wanting more....

*Available at your
favorite retail outlet.*

Silhouette Desire

presents

BEYOND BUSINESS

(SD #1649, April 2005)

by Rochelle Alers

The sizzling conclusion of

THE BLACKSTONES OF VIRGINIA

Seduction is on the agenda for patriarch
Sheldon Blackstone when he learns his new secretary
is sexy *and* expecting! A widower who never thought
he'd have a second chance at love, Sheldon must
convince the commitment-wary career woman to
trust her heart and begin a new family with him on
his sprawling, glamorous plantation.

Available at your favorite retail outlet.

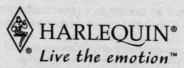

Susan Crosby

presents three brand-new books
in her tantalizing series:

*Where
unbridled
passions
are revealed!*

RULES OF ATTRACTION
(Silhouette Desire #1647, April 2005)

HEART OF THE RAVEN
(Silhouette Desire #1653, May 2005)

SECRETS OF PATERNITY
(Silhouette Desire #1659, June 2005)

Available at your favorite retail outlet.

Visit Silhouette Books at www.eHarlequin.com   SDBCDMINI

COMING NEXT MONTH

#1645 JUST A TASTE—Bronwyn Jameson
Dynasties: The Ashtons
When Jillian Ashton's arrogant husband died, it wasn't long before she found a man who treated her right—*really* right. Problem was, Seth—a tall, dark and handsome hunk—was her late husband's brother. She'd planned on just a taste of his tender touch, but was left wanting more....

#1646 DOUBLE IDENTITY—Annette Broadrick
The Crenshaws of Texas
Undercover agent Jude Crenshaw only meant to attract Carina Patterson for the sake of cracking a case against her brothers. But when close quarters turned his business into their pleasure, Jude could only hope his double identity wouldn't turn their new union into two broken hearts.

#1647 RULES OF ATTRACTION—Susan Crosby
Behind Closed Doors
P.I. Quinn Gerard was following a suspected accomplice—or so he thought. When the sexy bombshell turned out to be her twin sister, Claire, Quinn no longer had to watch her every move. But he couldn't seem to take his eyes off her! Could Quinn convince Claire to bend the rules and give in to their mutual attraction?

#1648 WHEN THE EARTH MOVES—Roxanne St. Claire
After Jo Ellen Tremaine's best friend died during an earthquake, she was determined to adopt her friend's baby girl. But first she needed the permission of the girl's stunningly sexy uncle—big-shot attorney Cameron McGrath. Cameron always had a weakness for wildly attractive women, but neither was prepared for the aftershocks of this seismic shift....

#1649 BEYOND BUSINESS—Rochelle Alers
The Blackstones of Virginia
Blackstone Farms owner Sheldon Blackstone couldn't help but be enraptured by his newly hired assistant, Renee Williams. Little did he know she was pregnant with her ex's baby. Renee was totally taken by this older man, but could she convince him to make her—and her child—his forever?

#1650 SLEEPING ARRANGEMENTS—Amy Jo Cousins
The terms of the will were clear: in order to gain her inheritance Addy Tyler needed to be married. Enter the one man she never dreamed would become her groom of convenience—Spencer Reed. Their marriage was supposed to be hands-off, but their sleeping arrangements changed everything!